HUDSON

THE MANNING DRAGONS BOOK 2

KATHI S. BARTON

This is a work of fiction. Names, characters, places, and incidents are products of the author's imagination or are used fictitiously and are not to be construed as real. Any resemblance to actual events, locations, organizations, or persons, living or dead, is entirely coincidental.

World Castle Publishing, LLC
Pensacola, Florida
Copyright © Kathi S. Barton 2017
Paperback ISBN: 9781629898087
eBook ISBN: 9781629898094
First Edition World Castle Publishing, LLC, October 2, 2017
http://www.worldcastlepublishing.com
Licensing Notes
Cover: Karen Fuller
Editor: Maxine Bringenberg

Chapter 1

Stop. Cooper stopped moving and waited for Carson to speak again. *To your left is a young woman. I want you to stick close to her for a bit. She's in danger, and you have to save her.*

Sure. And while I'm at this and she calls the police, will you bail me out of jail? I'm sure that she'll be thrilled to death to have a big hulking man standing close to her. Carson didn't seem all that amused at him, and he could almost taste her anger. *I'm sorry*

Look. I didn't ask for this shit. The least you can do is – When she stopped talking his dragon roared up around him. *Wait right where you are. I can feel...Cooper, in a few seconds, like five or less, this black car is coming around...Cooper, shield her. And Rose is with you.*

Pushing the woman and her burden to the glass front of the store they were near, he felt the bullets spray over them. Glass shattered around them. The mannequin in the window looked like it had been on the front line of a war, the way its body took the bullets. The pain took his breath away even as the squeal of tires sounded in the distance. Cooper heard

Rose telling him to not move, to stand still. Cooper felt the hot blood of his body running down his back, his legs too. The woman started to scream, and it hurt his already pounding head.

"Hush." Closing her mouth, she looked up at him, and he saw the baby cradled in her arms in some sort of carrier that strapped it to her. "The baby? Is it all right?"

"Yes, I think so. He's just afraid. So am I. You saved us." He just nodded, staring back at the little guy in her arms. He could hear Carson yelling at him, but he couldn't answer her just yet. Every part of his body ached.

"Cooper?" He looked at his brother by turning his head slightly. It hurt, and for the life of him, he couldn't remember his name. "Hudson. It's Hudson. I've called an ambulance, and the police are on their way too. Carson knows that I have you and that you're alive. Just don't move right now and we'll make sure that he's not returning to finish the job."

"I can do that, I think. Hudson, what happened? And the woman and her baby? Are they really all right?" Hudson said that he had her, and Cooper realized that at some point, he'd been moved and she and her baby were gone. "I hurt, Hudson. Help me."

"I am. Okay? You're going to be fine, I promise you. Just let me lower you to the sidewalk." Yes, he thought. That sounded really good. "Come on, buddy. Don't faint on me just yet."

"Okay." It was surreal. Blood was everywhere, and he was sure that it was all his. He looked up at the broken glass and then at his body. There were shards of it in his arms and shirt front. Putting out his hand, he was relieved when Rose landed on him. "I got hurt."

It seemed stupid to say that, but he really was hurting,

and he was also, he figured, in a little shock. As she sat down, watching him carefully, he began to feel just a little better. Not great, but better now that he was sitting.

"Yes, my lord. But you are not going to die. We saved you." He looked around the best he could. "They did their job for you, and I am very proud of them."

The other faeries were gathering their dead. His mind was still slightly fuzzy, his memory of them being with him all but gone. But he looked at Rose and she looked so sad. These were her men, and they had saved his life. He wasn't sure what had happened, not yet at any rate. So he looked to his faerie.

"What happened?" Rose told him that Carson had called them to him. "How did they save me, Rose? I need to know what happened that brought them to me."

"The spray of bullets was aimed at your heart and throat, my lord. The woman was the target, as was her son, but with you protecting them, neither of them were killed. The man, he'll be captured soon enough. The woman has minor damage, but she will heal. Had the bullets hit you in either place, they would have killed you with the amount of damage. The piercing of your heart with such a dagger as a bullet, or the spray of bullets going through your throat, would have removed your head. Many of your men, they gave their life for you today." He asked her how many there were. "Sixty-seven. There will be great mourning and celebrating today."

He knew that they would mourn their deaths…it would be hard on the families they left behind. And they would also celebrate the fact that they had saved his life. He'd do something for them, as would Rose. Too many deaths, he thought. And he'd be sure to take care of their families too. Cooper asked her to let him know what it was they needed and he'd make sure they had it.

He reached for Carson then. His heart was hurting from the loss, and he needed to connect with her to comfort him. She held his heart in her hands, and she would be the only one to help him when he was this down. He told her what had happened and that he was all right, thanks to her and his army.

Hudson told me. I'm on my way to you now. Christ, I'm so sorry. Tell Rose that as well. He said that he would, and for her to be careful. *I will. I love you. That man, he would have killed them both. I didn't feel the baby until it was almost too late. I'm so sorry. But he would have hurt them badly, Cooper. Thank you for putting up with me and doing this for them.*

I know, honey. I know that. And I'm glad that you did this. I don't know how either of us would have been able to stand by when we could do something. She was babbling, but it was all right. Carson had saved them, and him as well. Sirens were blaring, and he told Carson to head to the hospital, he'd see her there. *The mom and the baby are fine, thanks to you. You go there and I'll be there soon.*

"Cooper, you okay?" He nodded at Hudson. "I'm to stick with you like glue. Carson told me that I had to or else. And when she has an or else at the end of a request, I don't think I want to mess around with her. So we're stuck until she says differently."

"No, I'd not do that. I'm feeling a little better now. Thank you for being here for me and her. Rose lost so many men. I'll have to do something for them." Hudson sat on the sidewalk next to him when the medics went to check on the woman and baby. "What do you know so far? Whoever it was, he was aiming at them, not me."

"I know. Carson told me. Do you have a story?" He said

8

that he didn't, had not even thought about one yet. "You saw the car coming around the corner. Just that. Didn't know the man or the woman. Carson said less is more in this. She said to just say that you only had thoughts for keeping the woman safe, that's all."

Nodding at Hudson, he felt a little dizzy and decided to lay back. At the last minute, he turned to his side, so as not to cause any more pain in his back. The discomfort was manageable right now, but when the medics asked him about it, he knew that he had to be hurting worse than he was. Laying it on thicker than he felt, he told them he was in a great deal of pain, as well as his head hurt. He was moved to sit up to be examined by the medic when he came to him, and Cooper asked about the woman and her child.

"We have her, Lord Manning. She's just fine. So is her son. Thanks to you." The medic, he thought his name was Ben, laughed a little. "They caught up with her husband down the street a little ways. He is one pissed off man, I guess, because he missed her. What on earth would drive a man to try and murder his wife and son? If that don't beat all, I don't know what does."

"He didn't miss me." Ben said that he could see that, but he was able to take it better than anyone else. "True, but it didn't lessen the pain. What are we doing now? I'm assuming that I'm not just going to be patted on the head and sent home, am I?"

"No, sir, I'm afraid not. You're going in the ambulance when it comes. We sent the first one on site in with the baby and mom, just to be sure we didn't miss anything. Mom has a minor wound on her leg, nothing compared to you. I think I've counted twenty-two shots to you." Cooper asked if he was kidding. "Nope. Could be more. I've not looked at your back just yet. Probably more. But you're fine."

Cooper felt sick then. Twenty-two? Then he did just what his brother had told him not to do and fainted. Cooper felt the concrete beneath him bang hard against his thick skull, then he was out.

When Cooper woke he was in a hospital. Not that it surprised him, but he did feel heavy. Looking down his body, he knew why. The room was quiet, and he realized that he was alone. Sitting up, he stared at his left leg and the cast that was holding him down. He wondered if it was a joke or something.

It was a thick cast, and was being held up by some sort of crane like thing. His arm was also in a sling, but no cast. There was an ace bandage around it with blood stains on it, but he didn't think about that right now. Instead, he thought about getting out of there.

Just as he was ready to yell for help, Carson walked in the room and launched herself at him. As she sobbed about how sorry she was that he'd been hurt, Cooper assured her that he was fine, and better now that she was with him. Then he asked about the baby and his mom.

"They're fine. Debbie has a few stitches, but nothing that'll keep her down. The little boy, Robbie, he's perfect. I've been playing with him while the mom was being x-rayed. How are you?" Cooper told her he was fine, but looked down at his body again. "You scared the crap out of me when I lost the connection with you. Had Hudson not told me that you passed out, I might have torn into someone there. Are you really all right?"

"I promise you, I'm just fine. But, I need to ask, why do I have all this on me? I'm assuming for the police." She told him that the news stations were there as well. "I guess I understand, but it's a little much, don't you think?"

"No. I don't. They took a total of thirty-nine bullets out of you, Cooper. Thirty-nine. They could wrap you from head to toe if they wanted to." He laid his head back. Christ. "Rose lost some men. I told her whatever she needed, it was hers. Also, I asked her for a list of the names and their families. I thought we could do something for them. Okay?"

"Yes, of course. Flowers. They'll need flowers for the garden that they'll plant in their honor. It's been a while since we've had this many lost. I'm sure that Rose could use the help in any way we can give her. She knows all her men and their families. She will come to you. A task this large will need some helping. I know that it seems like an odd thing, but they'll need blankets too. They can use one of the ones in the cabinet, and they'll cut it down for themselves." Carson nodded. "What about the mom and baby? They need anything? I mean, that man, he wanted her dead in a powerful way."

"They'll need a place to stay. She said no, they'd be fine, but I've made it happen for her. I guess she was also looking for a job, which is also taken care of. We're going to take her to the distribution center when she is up and around." He liked that idea. "Babysitting is going to be an issue. Not because we don't have anyone, but because everyone wants to do it. Myself included."

"She have any family close?" She told him that she had a dad, and he was coming to be with her. She'd sent a car. "You are a wonder, my dear. Thank you for taking such good care of them both, and me."

"Debbie's husband, Robert Jersey, is in jail. He's being held on four counts of attempted murder, as well as a few other things, like firing a gun in city limits. His crew, as he calls them, are also being held without bond. Two of them are just kids, no older than Simon, who, by the way, is worried about you as well. So is John. They'll be in later." He asked her about the four attempts. "Well, Debbie and her son, you, and a clerk in the store was nearly killed as well."

"Okay, that makes sense. But thanks to you, everyone is all right. I hate to think what might have happened had you not been on top of things. I love you, Carson." She told him that she loved him as well. "When can I break out of here? I'm behind in stuff at home, and I feel fine. Please tell me that I can leave soon?"

She was shaking her head at him. "They're going to keep you a couple of days. For the press. And the boys want to come in to see you as well, as I said. Don't be surprised if they're a little standoffish. Remember, their mother died in this hospital." Cooper said he'd like for them to come, but if it was too much for them they could see him when he got home. "All right. They're here with your family now. They all need to see you. I think they got a good scare from this."

"So did I." Cooper found that he really needed to be with them too. His family meant the world to him. When the door opened a moment later, Cooper felt better. Just having them there made the inconvenience of the casts and being in the hospital much more tolerable.

~~~

Winnie heard her name called and went to the long tables that had been set up for job interviews. The man sitting behind it had a personality like a flea-bitten donkey, and he sort of had the look of one too. And Winnie so badly wanted to change his attitude. Or kill him. Either would make her feel better, but she needed a job.

He held out her application. "You didn't fill this out correctly. Go back and sit down and fix it before you can

12

move on to the next part of this process. If you pass, that is. I have final say in who gets to go to the next part of getting a job." She asked him what she'd done wrong. He jerked the form from her and turned to the second page. "It said mark what languages you know, not the ones you don't. So fix it."

Then he shoved it back at her so that she had no choice but to take it. The man was getting on her last good nerve, which she didn't have a lot of to begin with. Letting out a slow breath so she didn't snap, she worked on giving him her best smile.

"It's correct." She tried her best to hand it back to him, but he wouldn't take it. "I understood the question and I marked it correctly."

"You expect me to believe that you can speak seven languages?" Winnie said no. "Just as I thought. You need to—"

"There was only space for seven listed. I can speak twenty-three, including sign language." He looked ready to erupt and jerked it from her once again. "If you want, I can write those down too. I don't mind at all."

He tore her application in half. Winnie stood there for several moments, telling herself it wasn't worth it, nor was he, until she felt she was calm enough. Picking up her application, Winnie turned and made her way to the door. Fuck this shit. She'd have to more than likely murder someone else if she had to work there.

She'd been let out of prison yesterday, and had been told that she was to show up here and fill out an application. Well, she'd done that, all the way up to the very end of what she'd been told to do. But there was no way in hell she would try and appease an asshole, no matter how badly she needed to find something to do.

13

"Miss, you can't take that with you. You're supposed to turn it…What happened?" The woman had been at the other tables, the interview tables, when Winnie had come in earlier today. Winnie supposed she wasn't going to make it that far. "Come with me."

The intrusion in her mind started then. It wasn't painful, but very clumsy. Glancing at the other woman as they made their way to her table, Winnie figured that she had nothing to lose and spoke softly to her.

"You need more practice if you're going to enter peoples head and not have them know you're there." The woman stopped and stared at her. "Or you could just wait for someone to answer your questions. That's how I usually handle it. Then if that doesn't work, I flip into their mind. But that's just me."

"I've not had this shit long. I keep referring to it as magical shit, but it's kind of nice most of the time. And I'm sorry. I try hard to get better at it, and all I wanted to know was if you had been hurt by anyone here." Winnie said that she could see that, but she needed to work on it. "I got it when I got myself a mate."

"Did you want something? I can answer it if you don't try to get into my head again. I will hurt you." She didn't threaten the woman, but merely told her what she'd do. Surprisingly, she said that she'd not do it again. "Thank you."

"Donald, the guy at the application line, he pissed you off. Why?" Winnie shrugged. "He's pissed me off a few times as well. I think he won't be here tomorrow. Would you mind telling me what happened that your application ended up in several pieces?"

Winnie told her that it didn't matter now, just to forget it. "I don't think he's much of a people person. I mean, I do have a habit of pissing off people, but I didn't do it today. At least not to him. I need a job." The woman introduced herself. "Hello Carson, I'm Wendall Fitzpatrick. I go by Winnie."

"Wendall?" Winnie smiled at her, remembering her story that was as made up as her life history was, and the man who had made it up for her. "Oh, this must be good. Why is a beautiful woman like you named Wendall?"

"Dad had it in his head I was going to be a boy, I guess. And when my mom passed away just after I was born, he was so grief stricken that he didn't ask. So he filled out the birth certificate thinking I was his son. I guess it wasn't until a few days later that he figured it out. Needless to say, he wasn't happy." Carson asked if he was happy now with her. "I think he was. He was, I guess. He passed away a few months ago. You're very kind to talk to me. But I really need a job, and—"

"I'm hiring you." Winnie told her no, it was all right. They'd ended up back at the interview table by then, and when Carson sat down, so did Winnie. "I know that. It's why I'm hiring you. Tell me, what happened?"

"With Donald? He's a prick about my application and how I answered a few of the questions. It really doesn't matter."

Carson didn't ask her which ones, and Winnie didn't volunteer any information. Winnie just waited for her to ask about her stint in prison and what she'd done when Carson looked over her application. But she only put all the pieces in a folder and stood up from the table. Winnie figured she'd be shown the door now.

"Do you have a shift preference? I'd like to have you on days, where we can get the most use out of your talents, but we can work around whatever you need." Winnie was sure that she was joking…there wasn't any way she'd be hiring her. "Of course, perhaps we can get you on days that run over into a little bit of second shift too, if you can."

"Days is good. Did you read my application?" Carson said that she had. "No, you didn't. I mean, if you had, then you'd be walking me out, not asking about what shift I want. I have a record. Did you know that?"

"Yes, I saw that. I'm assuming that you've paid your debt to society and that you're very sorry." It was said with a huge grin that stumped Winnie. She told her that she had, and was sort of sorry. "Good. Now, I have a job for you. Supervisor of pick light. It's very easy to learn. I mean, if I can, anyone can."

"I think you're smarter than you let yourself know you are. But I murdered someone. Just pulled a knife out and cut him to shreds." When Carson asked her what he'd done to her first, Winnie stared at her. No one had ever asked her that before.

"You're intelligent, speak several languages. You're looking for employment, and you didn't lie to me. Did you?" Winnie said that she hadn't, but didn't think she could anyway, but that she was missing the point. "No, I don't think I am. Something happened, and you ended up on the wrong side of something. Or someone. Besides, everyone needs a second chance. Don't you think?"

Winnie followed her, her mind a tumble of questions. Mostly it was why Carson was taking such a chance with her. When they entered the office, she was shocked to her very core. Cooper Manning was there, and Winnie knew with certainty that she was in a new kind of hell.

"Lord Manning." Winnie looked at Carson, everything sort of falling into place now. "Carson Manning, I'm assuming."

"Yes, this is my wife." He didn't stand up. It was then that she noticed the baby in his arms. "I'm babysitting while his mom has a look around. Have a seat, Winnie."

16

"I'd rather not." He simply pointed to the chair across from him. "Please allow me to leave here. I'll not bother you again if you would do the same for me. Had I known that you were—"

"Sit down, Wendall." She did so, but was ready to run if the opportunity presented itself. "How's Patrick? I tried to find him."

"Dead." He told her he was sorry. "Are you? I did what I was told, and he was left alone. The man deserved to die, yes, and I killed him, but it cost me more than the five years of my life. And for what? So that you could go on with your life? Have your entire well-being just fine and dandy? You told me that I had to kill that man, then you left me there."

"I had you released, and had you sent here. I thought you'd enjoy your freedom a bit longer or we would have been prepared for your coming. I had assumed, sadly, that you'd spend some time with Patrick. I hadn't heard of his passing. For that, I am truly sorry. But—"

"Shove it up your fucking ass." She stood when he did, handing the baby off to Carson. He took a step toward her and she felt his dragon. "Kill me, as is your right. Kill me and end this. I won't fight you in any way."

Cooper paused mid-step, then asked her what she'd said. Telling him no, begging him to end her life, she braced herself for whatever he did. She would welcome it.

Winnie could fight back. Could hurt him and his dragon, even as depleted as her magic was. But she wouldn't. Dead was much preferable to living, to her.

"I cannot do that. I'm sorry, but I need you, and want you here. Your services have been needed for a long time, Winnie." She told him that she wasn't going to work for him, not ever again. "Yes, well, if I have to order you to help me, then I will. Lives depend on it too much for me to allow this to go."

"And what I want…as usual, my needs do not matter to you and your needs." He said that they did. "Nay, you will make me. That isn't what I want. I wish to be returned to prison. Now."

"Excuse me." They both looked at Carson when she spoke. "I don't have a clue what the fuck is going on here, but someone does need to explain to me what happened between the two of you so I can tell you how stupid you're being. And then we can move on to more important matters."

"Carson, love, this is Wendall Fitzpatrick, hit man for the Dragon Board. She has been around…well, nearly as long as me." Carson looked at her. "She would say she'd been cursed to be around me. She's told that to me enough times in my life. But she has saved more dragons than anyone, ever. And she ended up in prison when she, quite by accident, killed the wrong man."

"Because he told me to." Cooper nodded and smiled. "So I've been stuck in a fucking prison, where I was put when no one showed up at my trial to save me. And in the meantime, the man who was kinder to me than even my own parents ever were died of a broken heart."

"I'm sorry." She turned to leave, knowing that she couldn't stay, no matter what he said now. "The slayers are here. They're after my family. My brothers and my sons. We truly need you, Winnie."

"I don't care." Which was a lie, because she did too much, that was the problem. And it mattered little who this man was and what he'd done to her. "If I take care of this, will you never bother me again? Never in any way? And I do this my way."

18

"Deal." He'd agreed too quickly, and she turned to look at him. She knew there was more to this than a simple slayer. She didn't know what right now, but she had a feeling that she'd just been had. "My family would like for you to stay with us."

"No. I do this my way, and that does not include mingling with the Mannings." He nodded, as if he had figured she'd say that. Going out the door, she knew she was going to regret this, that she needed to have her head examined. Reaching out for help from anyone she could beg from, she wasn't surprised to have Rose answer her call. Winnie had wondered if the little warrior was still with Cooper, and now she knew. She just hoped that Rose would be helpful, and not report every little thing she did back to her boss.

Chapter 2

Finishing up the notes that he'd taken with the other family businesses, he made a final entry to his own file. He had all his things in neat files and labeled so that he could pull them easily without having to look up where he'd put them. Hudson liked to be organized, just as he loved having his thoughts in order. He was just closing up his computer when the door to his office opened and there stood Xavier, his baby brother.

"I need some advice." Hudson said hello to him and told Xavier that he might have an answer. "You will. It's about a building that I've just purchased downtown. You live there. It's the apartment complex. I bought it with good intentions, but I would like for you to help me out a little."

"I thought you had enough going on right now with buying the Ford house. Need a bigger challenge? But I didn't know it was up for sale, good job on that. What's the question?" Xavier told him his plans for the building. "So you want to tear it down and make it into bigger condos? I almost hate to admit this, because it'll mean I have to move, but that's

21

a good idea. The places are small and kind of outdated. Not to mention, there is little to no parking anymore. Not with everyone having more than one or two cars. Then there is the added fact that the condos will bring in a nice bit of cash for you. Very smart, little brother."

"Thanks. And that's what I noticed when I was there a couple of weeks ago when I was visiting you. I had to drive around for nearly an hour just looking for a space to park that didn't get me towed off. And it didn't really go up for sale so much as I was in the right place at the right time. Alan Peck was there filing some things for Lucas when it came up. He told me that it was going to go to auction if no one put in a bid by the end of the day. I won it for a very low-ball price." Hudson told him congratulations. "Yes, but this is where I need your help. I don't need to secure a loan or anything, I have the money, but I should borrow. I would like for you to go with me, just to be there so that I don't fuck this up legally and to keep me focused. I'm not stupid, but sometimes I don't see the bigger picture when the little ones keep distracting me. Understand? Nevertheless, the bank is doing some pretty nice things around town, and I think if they don't drum up more business, we'll have one of those bigger banks here that is as impersonal as the idiot that works for Carson. Have you met him?"

"You mean Donald?" Xavier nodded with a grin. "Yes, I've had the not so much pleasure of working with him last week when I got back. He's a dick weed, as Carson is so fond of calling him."

"Yes, that would be him. She wants me to go in and fire him today or tomorrow. I'm going to wait until tomorrow. I have to gird up my loins for dealing with him. He's sort of a fast-talking slick bastard, and will probably have me thinking that I need to be fired before it's done." Hudson laughed with his little brother. "Anyway, he lives in the building as well. Not that I care, but he will have something profound to say about me kicking him to the curb. I am doing this the legal way, but I don't want to have to deal with him twice in one week. Notices will go out in the morning too."

"You sound like you have your plate full for a few hours. What did you need for me to do with this? And before you ask, nope, I won't go there and do this for you. You wanted to help out. Well, here's your first job." Xavier said he had that part. "Then what else, pray tell, have you got up your sleeve? And yes, I'd be happy to go to the bank with you. I'll need to be looking into a house for myself now."

"Did you know that Cooper has hired someone? As a hit man? I mean, I guess he's been around for a long time…it's his job to do this or something, but he's brought this guy in to look for the slayer and kill him." Hudson said that he had heard it, but not a lot about the person. "Carson said that she wasn't thrilled about having this person come in, but with her and Cooper having those boys now, she thought it was a good idea."

"Simon, he told me last night when he came over for some help with his English homework that they were having fun at the new school, but they're freaked out about all the extra protection. I think he's a smart kid, by the way. No one told him there were people watching them. He figured it out on his own." Xavier told him that he'd talked to him about it as well. "I want them all to be safe. And we both know that as soon as this slayer guy finds out how much these guys mean to us, he's going to attack them first."

"I know there isn't much we can do other than protect them as this point, but to bring in a hit man…. I don't know, it seems a little over the top."

Hudson didn't speak for a minute. He'd been around longer than Xavier. And while he knew of the trouble that the humans had caused them before they'd become men, Xavier had never really witnessed it. Not as they had. "Look, I know where this person is going to be staying. Carson said they were going to provide him with housing and stuff until this is finished. How about after you get your work done tonight and I finish up here, we take a trip over there and talk to him? That way you can see what sort of person he is...you know, trustworthy and such. Cooper would never hire anyone without knowing their worth, you know that. Then ask him what his plans are for this slayer person." Xavier said he liked that idea and told him he'd be back in a few hours, around dinnertime. "All right. I should be about done here as well, and we'll get us some dinner then be ready to go."

Getting things done was a lot easier than he thought it would be after talking to his brother. Sometimes he'd have something to do later and wouldn't get as much done as he wanted. He supposed it was in anticipation of doing something different. But today, he didn't have that problem. Work, for him, was as usual.

When he saved his work then closed up his computer, he had about thirty minutes before Xavier was to show up, so he went to the balcony off his office. He loved it there, and wished that he had the same view from his apartment. But that wasn't anything he'd worked very hard in making a reality. So now he had the opportunity to find himself a home by being forced out of his place. A real home with the kind of views he wanted. Instead of going back in the office, Hudson sat in one of his old lawn chairs and pulled out his phone and started looking for houses on the Internet. It was as good as any place to start.

By the time Xavier showed up again, he had four houses that he liked, and one of them was fairly close to his offices here, as well as his family. Hudson loved his family, and needed to be near them like he needed his next breath. He supposed a little of it had to do with them being dragons of the same family, but he loved them.

Hudson asked his brother about the houses. It seemed that he had a good idea about all four of them.

"The first house you have there is way overpriced. I've looked it over in searching for comparable prices for my home. There isn't a lot of land with it, not nearly as much as either of us would like, and the house needs a lot of repairs. I think that I'd skip that one all together." He asked about the second and third. "I'd look them over, but not buy for that price. If you'd like, I can go in and see what kind of deal I can get for you. I have an in with a couple of realtors."

"I don't want to know what that means." Xavier laughed and said he wouldn't tell him anyway. "And the last house? What is your opinion of it? The listing says that it has a lot of land, but not how much there is."

"I didn't see it in my searches. But I can tell you that it's in a good neighborhood. I like that it has a bit of acreage coming with it. I think, if I remember the place at all, it had a greenhouse or something on it at one time." Hudson pointed out that he'd said he didn't think he knew much about it. "I love to walk around the wooded areas around town. I don't know the house, but the land I do know. It's a beautiful piece of property. And for that price? I think I'd buy it if I didn't have my own home already. But again, I could maybe get you a better deal."

"Do it then. I'll pay asking, but if you can do me better,

then go for it. And anything you need with your project, let me know. I'll even finance mine, as I said, to help out around the town." Xavier thanked him. "All right. How about we get some dinner, then go to see this man? It's not far from town, and that way if this person turns out to be a dud, we'll just go home and not worry about it anymore."

"All right, but since this was my query, I'm buying." Hudson told him that he'd not have it any other way. "Thanks. You can leave the tip. That's the least you can do for the town."

It was going to be fun, Hudson thought, hanging with his brother. Going to see this man, whoever he was, probably wasn't going to be leaving any kind of impression on either of them. He had no idea why he thought that, but it was in his head. So, they were seated in the restaurant and given menus, and Hudson promptly pushed the man and his job out of his head.

~~~

Rose moved around the house with her. It wasn't that big...a couple of bedrooms and a kitchen-dining room area. She had a bathtub, something that she had missed, and a nice sized shower stall that she could use too. It was private, another thing that she'd missed while being cooped up. To take a shower alone would be heaven, she thought.

The garage had been converted into one of the bedrooms, so it was large by any standard, but she thought that she'd use the smaller one as her sleeping area and the bigger room as her office. Besides, the garage was the perfect size for the exercise equipment that she wanted to bring in and use too. All in one area suited her just fine.

"I'll need some gym equipment...a bike if you can find one, as well as a rowing machine. Weights too, if you can find them." Rose said she'd make sure they were ordered. "I can

26

put them together, so don't opt for that. I don't want anyone in here other than those that have to be. Also, don't buy new. I don't want to have to deal with the boxes or whatever that comes with them, and I won't be here long enough to get much in the way of wear and tear on the things."

"There is a cook should you wish. She is wolf, and I'm told she's quite good at it." She told her that she didn't eat much anymore and wouldn't require a cook. "As you wish, my lady."

"Don't call me that. I'm not that person anymore." Rose said nothing, but Winnie felt that she had to clarify what she meant. "That was all taken from me the day I entered the prison. And anyone else that works with this thing, they're to call me Winnie or nothing at all."

"Yes. All right." They went through the rest of the house. A few things needed to be taken care of. Security for the most part. But she also found that the basement was only a shell of a place, and asked if she could get the doors locked from the inside and out. "The house is for you to do with as you wish. As Cooper said, you are doing this your way."

Winnie didn't say anything. If she had her way, which she rarely did, then she'd be dead about now, not keeping house for herself. There were boxes of new items laying in each room. Sheets and pillowcases. The bathroom had several boxes of things as well. Towels, toiletries, and a few other personal items. Winnie wondered who had picked them out, and decided that she didn't care. This was only temporary.

She also had a car, a Jeep, to use. It was four-wheel drive as well as bullet proof. There were other extras on it as well, things that again she wondered who had ordered them. More than likely Cooper had remembered her preference for things to be stashed in and under the cars she drove and had it outfitted for her. They were back in the house a few minutes later, and all Winnie could think about was her father.

James Fitzpatrick wasn't really her dad. Her own had been gone long ago, so long ago now that she didn't remember his face. She'd never heard what had taken him and her mother, but she really didn't care. They were gone from her life, and that was just the way she liked it.

Known as Patrick to his friends, she'd adopted his name as her last so people wouldn't ask him how he'd come to have a long-lost daughter. She'd been just Wendall until then. And over the ensuing years, he'd become her friend as well as someone, probably the only person, that she could depend on to be there when she needed them. Then, Cooper had failed her on his part in getting her out of serving jail time.

Her own father had been an abusive bastard. Her father's hand...she remembered that, and the way that he'd smack her every time she did something he didn't approve of. There were plenty of those times, too. Her mother had been something of an addict; not to drugs or anything, but to her mate. Winnie's mother and father were as close if not closer than most sister and brothers she knew. They never strayed far from each other, and couldn't care less what she'd been up to.

Then she'd met the Dragon Board. It had been a meeting of minds, she supposed now. Winnie had found out that they were looking for a dragon that had been in a great deal of trouble. It had only taken her a few days to search him out and bring the rogue to them. The reward, she found too late to refuse, had been not money, which she wanted, but magic. And a great deal of it.

Her parents had been horrified that she'd been given magic, then jealous of the attention that she'd gotten by working for the Dragon Board to help with the capture and killing of rogue dragons. That was what made her never return home at such a young age and never look back. She was sure that they hadn't either. But Winnie had stayed true to herself and worked hard.

"My...Winnie? I have something else for you." She looked at the tiny faerie and asked her what it was. "It's magic. Your own, as well as a little more."

"How did you...? Where did you get it? It was taken from me when I was put behind bars. They didn't want me escaping, I guess. Not that I would have tried. But that's...You really do have my magic?" Rose nodded and asked her if she wanted it now. "Who authorized for you to have it?"

"Lord Cooper had it given to him to return to you. He had to convince them that you were the only one for the job that he needed you for." Winnie didn't believe that any more than she did that Cooper wasn't responsible for her being in jail anyway. She might be able to do the job, it was yet to be seen, but Cooper hadn't cared for her then, and Winnie doubted that he did now. "Would you like it now?"

The doorbell rang, and before the chimes of it were finished, someone pounded on the door. There was a sense of urgency there, one that gave her a little twinge of unease. But Rose asked her again if she would like it now.

"Yes, I am, but not the extra stuff. I don't want anything from him." Rose smiled, but the door was being pounded on again. It was starting to piss her off. "I'll be back."

Winnie decided that she was going to murder the person or persons on the other side of her door. She didn't have any idea why they were in such a hurry to get in, but they'd pay for it. The doorbell, while sounding slightly sluggish, should have been enough for them. The pounding was just over the top.

Rose told her that it was hers just as she touched her fingers to her forehead. The touch was warm, and since Rose was such a tiny thing, it surprised Winnie how consuming it was. Heat filled her body, then coolness. Before she could think about what was going on, Winnie touched the door as it opened, and she cried out when she fell backward, barely able to stand on her own.

The pain now, it was almost unbearable. And before she could tell the men there that they couldn't touch her, she felt their hands on her body and felt their pain parallel her own. It was their party, she thought. You barge into a home unwelcomed, then you had to pay the price somehow. She knew they were going to suffer much like she was, and Winnie thought it was funny. And painful.

If they were human they'd be dead, she thought. It was too late for the men; they'd either be over powered and die or they'd just die. Right now, however, she had her own set of problems to deal with. Then the world tilted around her once again. She felt sick to her stomach just as her body became whole.

Her wings that she used to get someplace quickly filled her back. The magic of them was there, just enough that she recalled how much she had missed them. There were other pieces of her armor too; her boots that protected her legs and feet, armor across her chest. The gloves too, to keep her hands from being cut should she have to get into a sword fight. Her beloved sword, one that had been given to her more years ago than she could even remember. And it had served her as well as the dragons she'd sworn to protect.

She'd gotten the more, the magic that she'd told Rose she didn't want. It was racing over her body like a freight train without brakes. The more it entered her body and bloodstream, the faster it seemed to take her. The magic that had been kept from her was now a part of her again.

Falling to her knees, then her belly, she glanced at the men and saw that they were dragons. Whatever had happened to them, their beasts had come out. Curling into a tight ball, trying her best to deal with all that was moving in her, Winnie cursed Cooper Manning and his fucking family.

She didn't pass out, mores the pity, but laid there feeling every inch of herself. The hair on her body seemed to have a life of its own, and she could hear it moving. Her teeth shifted in her mouth as her fangs, another gift from the Board, grew in her mouth. Winnie's back itched, and she knew that her wings, her favorite part of her, needed to be stretched out, to fly in the sky like they were meant to do. Soon she'd be her old self again, with a few extras.

"What the fuck was that?" She heard the man but didn't have the strength to answer him. The dragons had taken their bodies back, she realized, and closed her eyes. Rose answered him, she thought, as he spoke again. "What do you mean, I'm evolving? Into what? And where the hell did that come from?"

"You touched her." The man, this time the other one, asked why that should matter. "Because she was getting her powers back and you touched her. Did you not hear me say to not touch her? I don't know what this is going to do for you."

"It's not going to do anything because you're going to fix this." Rose told the first man that she could not, he'd done it. "I was helping a woman that looked to be in distress. And this is what I get for it? Oh, no, this is not going to be happening."

"Well, it is, Lord Hudson. Now, lie still while it works over you." He must have not heeded her advice, because the next time Rose spoke, she sounded very pissed off. "All right, but it is upon your head if you should fall to your face. I will not take responsibility for your folly."

The door slammed as he left and Winnie heard laughter. It wasn't the faerie, because it was decidedly masculine. Winnie didn't bother checking. She no longer cared who was in the house or if they went on a killing spree. She hurt too much.

"Miss, are you all right?" She told the man that she was fine. "My name is Xavier Manning. My brother hired this guy to come and help us out with a problem. Is he the one that did this to us?"

"No, that would be me on both counts. I'm the man your brother hired, and I'm the one that got the magic started. You shouldn't have touched me." He said he was beginning to believe that. "I don't know what we got, but I'd say quite a bit. And since you're a dragon, I'm clueless at how much more you're going to have. I guess it sucks to be you guys."

She rolled over and looked at the man. He was handsome if you went for that sort of thing. Big arms, tightly pulled back hair. She figured that he had to be related to Cooper, and didn't feel the least bit sorry for him hurting. When she could sit up, she did so and regarded the man across the room from her.

"I'm Wendall. Winnie is what I'm called." He told her his name again. "Cooper, he's your brother?"

"Yes. Hudson and I came over to talk to this guy...well, you I guess. We weren't so sure that hiring you was such a good idea. Not that we didn't think the guy—you—could do it, but I wondered at the need for a killer." She asked him how many slayers he'd encountered in his lifetime. "Two, and one of them was recent, but he died in his cell. We think he was murdered but arranged like he'd hung himself, but we can't get by the magic there."

"Slayer. He must be a strong one too. This other guy, the dead guy, you know his name?" He told her. "Yes, underling to a slayer. The name, it rings a bell, but I'll have to figure it out on my own. There was a Ford a while back, but I thought he'd died."

"There was a book. My sister-in-law, Carson—she can feel things now—she knew that he had it at one time. And knows that the book was in the house at one point, but it's disappeared now. We don't know what happened to it from the time that Ford was arrested until now. It seems to have disappeared." Winnie had heard of the book all her life. But the kid here—and he was a kid to her—he wouldn't have ever seen it. "You think that killing this man is the only way out of this?"

"I'm to understand that you have some humans in the household." He said his two nephews. "Do you have any idea what this guy will do to them, once he is able to snatch them? First he'll cut them down to nothing more than a stump. Arms and legs will be removed from them. In the event that they might think about running away, he takes that out of the equation. Then he'll have them read some messages. Nothing much, but a few well-placed words here and there. A sentence or two with them screaming too. Then he'll remove their tongues. No yapping when he's trying to think. After that, he'll—"

"All right. I get it. He's a bad mother fucker. So what are you going to do?" She was going to tell him but he stood up, speaking as he did so. "Never mind. I don't think I want to know. If you could say those other things without so much as a shiver, I would prefer not to know what it is you'll do to him."

"No, I'm reasonably sure that you don't. I don't play well with others." He nodded and stood over her. He asked if he could touch her now. "Yes, the damage is done, as they say. But I'm not ready to get up just yet. I like it here, on the floor, for now."

"All right. But since you're here working for us, if you need anything, or think of anything, call us. I'm sure that you have our numbers." Winnie didn't point out that they had a connection now, and she wouldn't need something as mundane as a phone. "I'll see you around, I guess."

"He is not like the others." Winnie asked Rose what she meant by that after Xavier left them. "He is younger than them, not only in years, but in violence awareness as well. When his father was killed by sharing the magic of the witch, they were too focused on blending in with the humans. It saved their lives to be a part of the human world, yes, but they were never very fond of them. Young Xavier, he never knew the troubles that the others grew up with."

"What did he mean by not even shivering when I talked about what a slayer would do to the kids?" She only stared at her from across the room. "He doesn't have any idea what I really am, does he? Do any of them? Besides Cooper?"

"I'm sure that the two you touched will figure it out soon enough, don't you think?" She asked her what she meant. "They are a part of you. The magic, the extra, they will be as much a part of your mind as you are."

Cursing, she stood up. Rose, probably sensing her anger, left her there. Would there never be an end to the shit that Cooper did to her? Would she ever be able to be her own person? Not now, it seemed. Now she had two more people in her head that would need to be blocked as much as she could. Winnie was going to have to work very hard in not murdering the men.

Chapter 3

Hudson looked over the house again. He already loved it, and was glad that he was going to be able to get a great deal on it. It was much bigger than he'd thought it was. Having a full finished basement with its own entrance, as well as a four-car garage, made it perfect for him. And the view was spectacular.

Xavier had called him after he'd left the house to tell him that his realtor friend would knock a nice sum off the house if he paid cash. While he wanted to help the town, the difference in price on it was too good to ignore. Now, four days later, here he was, standing in his own house.

Xavier was in the front hall when he came down the long staircase. "Congratulations. I heard that you bought yourself a home." Hudson told him that he had. "I like it here too. And you can't beat the acreage you got. Buying both of the lots that the seller owned was wonderful."

"Yes, I'll have to work on filling the rooms with some furniture now. But I don't have anything going on right now, and with it being too cold to go to auctions and estate sales, I'll be able to get it cleaned up and painted." Xavier went into the large kitchen with him. "This is nicer than I thought it would be too. I mean, they must have spent a fortune on updating this room alone. Everything here is high end."

"The dining room too, I guess. I heard that the cabinets alone were shipped from France and installed. I'm sorry that they didn't get to finish this place, but glad for you. Did you know about the fireplace?" He told him that the realtor had told him it needed to be cleaned. "I am so jealous, I have to tell you. But on a different note, the apartment residents are going to have three months to move out. I hope. The letters go out tomorrow."

"That was fast." He didn't want to talk about the woman, but he'd been having strange thoughts. Mostly about Cooper, and he needed to ask Xavier about it. He knew that his brother had left well after he had, but he didn't know if he'd talked to her. "This thing with the woman. Do you know any more than what we were told when I left there? I mean, what's the deal with it?"

Xavier sat down on the window seat that was in the dining room. "She said that she was the hitman. Winnie is her name, I guess. And the magic that we got, it's part of hers and a little more. I'm not entirely sure what that means, but I figured as a dragon, it won't be that bad. I have to tell you, Hudson, I was sick as a dog when I left her. Did you get it too?"

"No, I was exhausted, but not sick after that. Maybe I didn't get as much or something." Xavier said he didn't know, but he was glad that it turned out to be nothing. "Me too. And why a woman? I don't mean to sound chauvinistic or anything, but she's almost too beautiful to be considered anything but a model. Don't you think?"

"Perhaps that's the point." Hudson didn't care for what

36

that implied. And honestly, he wasn't sure why it bothered him. "Anyway, I told her if she needed anything to give us a call. She told me what a slayer would do if he got the boys. I don't know if she was being dramatic or what, but it's not good."

"I know what he'll do with them, Xavier. He'll make them suffer in ways I bet that she can't even imagine." Xavier told him what she'd said. "Okay, maybe she can. And she's not being over dramatic. I've heard of that being done to others. It's a common way to deal with humans when they know a dragon."

"I don't want to even think of that, not with the boys. I don't want to think of that for anyone, but with them, they're family." Hudson agreed and changed the subject by asking him about his home. "I'm having some work done now on the house. It's coming along nicely. There are things that I'm learning about owning a house that never come up. But I'm having a good time."

They both walked around the yard then. There wasn't much to do with it either. It would need to have the flower gardens redone, and he'd have to have some of the wood that had fallen in the storms this fall removed as well. The fireplace would get some nice usage with all of it. Xavier asked him if he was going to look at the greenhouse at the back of the property.

"You have time to go with me?" He said that he didn't have anything going on right now, and they headed there. "I don't know a great deal about greenhouses, do you? I mean, I know what they're used for, but I don't know that I'd have any use for it."

"Maybe your mate will." They both laughed about that, and the woman, Winnie, popped into Hudson's head at that moment. "Christ, Hudson, it's fucking huge."

It was too. He'd bet that a football field would fit nicely in it and have room left over on each side and the ends for the players to stand. It was made of glass, old glass that had bubbles in the panels, and the wood had been taken care of too. As soon as they entered the grand building, he knew he was going to have to find someone to use it, just so he could come out here and walk around the place.

"You should make yourself a roadside stand in the summer months and sell stuff you can grow in here. You'd make a killing, I bet."

They were both laughing when he realized that he really wanted to make it work. As the plan began to formulate in his head, he felt the twinge of something else, another person. "Do you feel that?"

"Yes, I think it's Winnie. She's...I think she's pissed off." Yes, he could feel that as well. And whoever she was pissed off at, they weren't going to survive if she didn't calm down. Xavier seemed nervous when he asked him the next question. "What do you think we should do?"

"I fucking don't know." Xavier laughed at him, and Hudson felt better as he continued. "It's like she has opened her heart and mind to us. I can feel her anger, and almost taste her patience too. She is mad, but working hard at not killing this person."

"I don't feel that part." Hudson only nodded, concentrating on what she was thinking. "Hudson, I don't know what you're doing, but I don't think I'd fuck with this person. She's really scary mean. I mean, like scarier than Cooper when he's in a bad mood."

What the fuck do you want now? Blood? If so, you'll have to wait your turn. Hudson was shocked at the amount of anger he felt from her. She didn't so much as speak to him, but screamed at him from her mind.

He asked Xavier if he could hear her too. After shaking his head, Xavier said he was leaving. When the shit hit the fan, he told him, Xavier didn't even want to be in the same state as him. So Hudson was left standing there while she yelled at him again.

Do you have a death wish, fuck head? He told her that he didn't. *You're one of those guys from the other day, aren't you? The one that left in a huff because he got knocked on his ass.*

Yes, that would be me. You're Winnie. Her anger doubled then, like dealing with him and the other person was taking its toll on her. *Can I help you?*

Help me what? Do you have any idea how stupid some people can be? I have this delivery guy here, flirting with me like I'm some sort of fish market buy, and all I want to do is cut him in half, then step over his dead body and get the rest of my things from the truck. Laughing might not have been the smartest thing he could have done, but it was funny for him. *What the fuck did you want bothering me? I have shit going on here.*

Ask the guy if his name is Charlie. If it is, tell him that I said for him to go home to his four children and his wife and leave you the fuck alone. Hudson sat down on one of the many benches that were along the wall of his greenhouse. *He also has three of those little yippy dogs. I want to have one for a snack every time I go over there.*

I hate dogs. Especially the kind that fit into a small purse. Why do people buy those things anyway? Give me a good-sized dog and I'm happy. Or a wolf, one that will eat anyone that comes to the door. Hudson was enjoying himself, and could feel her anger sliding away. *You more than likely saved old Charlie's life. He doesn't take no well, does he?*

More than likely the reason he has four children all under the age of ten. Did he at least leave you your packages? She said that she'd had to bring them in the house, but she had them. And thanked him again. *If you need help putting them together, whatever it is, I don't have anything going on right now. I could help.*

Don't push your luck, buddy. I just told you, I don't care for people at my doors. He laughed and she did as well. *I have no idea what is going on here, but it's nice. Not a habit forming nice, but okay. I have to get this set up. Don't be a pain in the ass about this.*

I won't be. Hudson made his way to the house and walked around again. *By the way, I'm Hudson. Cooper is my brother.*

I know who you are. And don't bother me. I have shit going on. He told her he was sorry and felt the connection close. When he closed his eyes, Hudson was surprised to see what she was seeing. *What the fuck is that now?*

I don't know. But I can see the instructions to your new computer in your hands. You have on a yellow tee shirt that has seen better days, and a pair of orange shorts. Not a good combination. And the boxes that you got are now — She told him to stop. *All right. But this is sort of freaking me out a bit.*

You? Christ, this is all I need. Some asshole dragon fucking around in my head. Hudson didn't take exception to being called an asshole because he was afraid. Not of her, but what he was seeing through her eyes. *Where are you now? I see you in a yard that is surrounded by snow. There is a house too, big sucker, that has dark shutters on it. And in the back, I see a barn or something.*

My home. And it's a greenhouse, not a barn. But I'm planning to put one in. She told him that she didn't give a good flying fuck. *Yes, well, I was helping you.*

40

There is no help for this. Can that other one see this too? I don't see him there, but can you ask him? He said he would and asked Xavier. After talking with him for several minutes, he got back to Winnie. If he was honest with himself, he was having a lot of fun. *He said no. He can feel your anger and now your confusion, but not see anything. I had him try it with his eyes closed too.*

Now what? Hudson had a feeling that she wasn't necessarily asking him, so he kept his mouth shut, but all kinds of things were in his head. Mostly things that he wasn't sure why they were there. *I can read your mind, dumbass. And that isn't helping. And we aren't ever going to do those things. I'm not going to be here long enough, if I have anything to say about it.*

Really? Because all I can think about is finding you and stripping you down to your luscious bare skin and tasting every inch of you. I don't know why, but it has me as hard as stone. She told him to shut the fuck up. *Yes, well, I'm not technically speaking anyway, so I've done that.*

Her growl was as tantalizing as his thoughts. Hudson found himself standing next to his truck then with his keys in hand. To go to her would be a mistake, he was aware of that, but at the moment, he couldn't think of anything else but to do just that. As soon as he was pulling out of his new driveway, he thought about why he had such a powerful need for her.

Christ. She told him she'd figured it out too. *You're my mate. Mother fuck, you're my mate, and a killer.*

Well, la-de-da for you. Yeah, I'm a killer, but you're a prick. You come here and I will hurt you, rules or not. You understand me? Come here and it will be the last thing you ever do. He believed her and pulled to the side of the road to think. *This is all Cooper's fault, and when I see him, I'm going to make sure he understands that this is not going to happen.*

Hudson was sure that it was too late for that. Right now

41

he had a mate that was pissed off at him, and he understood her reasoning. But for the life of him, he couldn't see how any of this was going to resolve anything. Hudson decided that he wasn't going to give his brother a heads up, and headed to his apartment to pack, and clear his head. Some things, he imagined, would be better had he just stayed home last week.

~~~

Ross walked around the house again. There had to be something here he was missing. The book, for one thing…the other was a safe, or perhaps a hidden floor board that could be removed. But Ford had told him that he didn't know where the book was, and he believed him. There had been nothing in his head when he'd visited him.

"Well, I killed him, not just a friendly visit." He glanced at his faerie and noticed that he wasn't paying attention as much as he thought he should. Snapping his fingers made the creature scream in pain, yet he seemed to have straightened up again. "When I am speaking, you are to listen to me. Do I make myself clear?"

"Yes, my lord." The creature had a name, he supposed, but all he ever called faeries was speck. "Will you require me to go through the house again?"

"Did you look as hard as I told you to do? Or did you slack off as you have been today?" He said that he'd spent the entire day looking for the book. "And is that any fault of mine? Had you come here when I told you to, perhaps I'd have it by now."

"Yes, my lord." Ross loved the fear that was there. The sound of it simply made his heart sing. If he had one, that was. "I will go and search the lands here. And return."

Nodding, Ross thought of his book. And it was his. The other people had only been holding it for him until he

42

reached his power. It had taken him much longer than he'd thought it would, but he was now stronger than anyone…the most feared creature that had ever been made. Or he would be soon enough, he thought. And he would be stronger still when he had his book.

The book. It seemed like such a simple thing. Pages bound and sewn together with something and magic put within it. He also knew that it would take a dragon to open it, one that was strong of heart and mind and of pure blood. That was the hardest thing he'd been trying to find. Dragons, like other creatures, would fuck whatever they could and breed themselves out of existence. Like the Manning ones.

The oldest one, Cooper, was proclaimed to be the best and smartest king ever born. Then he found himself mated to a human, of all things. And instead of killing her off and waiting for the next mate to come to him, he had not only married her, but had brought human children into his household. He'd soon take care of that too.

And the book was no simple one either. The cover had the skin of a faerie, its colors so brilliant that when held by the king, it would light the night. The pages were bound with the hair of a troll, the strongest kind of thread to use, even today. The ink was the blood of a vampire that had given it freely. Inside was dried dragon flesh that kept it locked, and the black magic of a witch was what kept it hidden from humans.

"Now all I must do is find my book, take it to the beast, and have him open it. Should be simple enough, don't you think?" He looked around for his speck and saw that he'd left him. Remembering at the last minute that he'd gone out to look for his book, Ross went to the window and looked out. "Stupid thing is more than likely looking in the snow for it."

The house was sold as of last week. He'd thought about

buying it for himself, but he'd been busy searching the house and hadn't gotten his bid in. But when he went to inquire about it, the banker had told him that the house had been sold with the payment of back taxes and fees. Such a small amount for it too, Ross had thought.

The car pulled into the drive a few minutes later. Pulling his magic around him, Ross hid in the corner of the large room and waited. Perhaps it would be someone that he could use for a time and have more energy. But as soon as the man walked into the house, he knew him for what he was. A dragon.

The man/dragon moved through the lower rooms while talking into a small device. Ross thought it was a recorder, and wondered if he could get one for himself. He was forever forgetting tasks that he'd set his speck on, and it would be helpful to remind the thing what he'd been told to do. As the man-made notes on what the kitchen needed, the speck came into the room too.

"Well, hello there." The speck looked at him, then back at the dragon. "You must be new around here. I don't remember ever seeing you before."

"I am new here, yes." Fear...it was almost like a fine dessert as it rolled off the thing. "I have nothing to tell you."

"I didn't ask you anything. Are you all right?" Speck nodded, but it wasn't convincing, apparently. "I know some of your kind. If you need help, I can assist you. What's your name?"

"My name?" Speck glanced at Ross, then back at the dragon again. "I am Barbed, your lordship."

"Hello. My name is Xavier. Xavier Manning, as a matter of fact. Are you taken?" Ross moved closer to the dragon and his property. The next few seconds would be the last the creature or the dragon ever had if things didn't go as he planned. "I claim you as my own, for now and all of eternity."

Ross felt the disconnection from his creature like a slap in the face. He wasn't sure how the dragon had done it and done it so quickly, but he was going to take the thing back from him. But Speck or Barbed moved to the dragon and sat upon his shoulder, whispering in his ear like they'd been together forever. When the man turned and looked at him, Ross felt the first finger of fear that he'd ever had.

"You're not supposed to be here." Ross didn't say anything but stood still. If he had to use his magic, it would give away what he was. And a slayer this close to a dragon would be a dead slayer. "You should be on your way. And this speck, as you called him, is mine."

"I need him." Xavier only crossed his arms over his massive chest and stared at him. "It is forbidden to take something magical from someone else. You know that law as well as me."

"I do, but you also need to claim him. Apparently you didn't, or I'd not have been able to do so. So, he is mine." When the man smiled, Ross realized what he'd done. "You know a great deal about my kind, don't you? I mean, you are trying hard to portray yourself as a human, when we both know that you are not. I don't know what you are, but you're not human."

Ross simply disappeared. Standing in his own home, he had to figure out what had happened. The dragon would know who he was now, and what was worse, the speck would tell him everything that he'd been up to since coming here. And he'd bet anything that the thing not only knew where the book was, but was not giving it to him.

Pacing now, letting his mind drift over what he'd been caught at, Ross realized that it might not be as bad as he had first surmised. First of all, the speck knew only that there was a book. He didn't know what sort of book it was, because he'd not thought him trustworthy enough nor smart enough to have been told.

Secondly, the dragon was big, but that wasn't something that should have scared him. He was bigger than he looked as well. Ross let himself shift in his skin, and felt the tightness of the house as he spread out.

Thirdly, and this should have been first, the dragon didn't know shit. Ross might have disappeared from the house, but a great many other creatures could do that as well. Vampires could, as well as faeries and brownies.

"I have worried for nothing. I am a slayer, and have been one for more years than that dragon has been living." He wasn't sure that was true, but right now he was boosting himself, not taking himself down. "And with the power that I have, I could have easily killed him, but didn't want to at that moment. It would have brought the others to me, and as I don't have the book, I cannot have them coming to me."

He felt better after just talking to himself. He did that a great deal, spoke to himself and worked things out aloud. There was a time when he would have bounced his ideas off someone else, but people, even creatures such as himself, would never understand the way his mind worked. And Ross knew that his was a far superior mind than anyone else's.

It wasn't something that he simply told himself either. He knew that he was smart. He was a great dragon killer too. In his lifetime, Ross knew for a fact that he'd killed more than a hundred of the creatures. And he'd sold off more of their magic than he'd kept, too.

It had been funny to him, when he was low on cash, to have sold the dead of some other deceased animal to unsuspecting people. A bone or two here, a bit of shiny rock to someone else. He'd even gone so far as to keep a bag of pretty shells in his home to sell off as scales.

"If they were stupid enough to think that a dragon's scale was that small, then they deserved to be cheated, don't you think?" He'd forgotten that he was alone again. "I'll need to find me another speck, and soon. This one I will have to claim."

Claiming a speck was the same as taking a mate. He'd have to care for it and not harm it in any way. That was why he'd stopped claiming them in the first place. The rules governing them had been too confining when he wanted to have a bit of sport. Ross thought he was well and good rid of the speck that the dragon took. He was beginning to wear on his nerves a little.

"No matter. In the morning, I shall go out and find another. They're as easy to find as the dragons were." Ross laughed. It was becoming fun now that he'd met one of the dragons. It would be easier still now that he knew what they looked like. "I think I'd like to play with them a bit. Yes, I think I shall."

That night when he went to his bed, he felt better than he had in ages. The dragons were out there, and they were as stupid as he'd ever known them to be. For something so large and strong, they were quite dumb, and gullible. He was going to enjoy this taking of them. As soon as he found the book, he was going to be the most powerful being in all of the worlds. And he would find it too. It was as simple as taking candy from a babe.

Chapter 4

The computer was doing its thing when her doorbell rang. Winnie was beginning to hate the thing. Every day someone would come by and ask her if she needed anything. Or did she want any help. Today she had already seen four such people, and she wasn't getting a damned thing done. Upon jerking open the door, Winnie took a step back when she saw who was there. Cooper didn't seem to be in any better of a mood than she was.

"Xavier saw him." Cooper came into the room before she could tell him to go away. "He was as close as you and I are right now, and he knew what he was. Isn't it your job to find this guy and kill him for us?"

"Is it? And good for him. So, if that's all you came over here for, I knew that already. Good-bye." The urge to hit him was great…like her arm and hand burned to do so. "He's here, you knew that when you hired me. And in a town this small, how did you think you weren't going to encounter him at least once or twice?"

"You should have killed him by now." Winnie thought of all the trouble she'd be in if she killed the dragon king. "Why are you looking at me like that?"

"Because, I don't know if you've noticed this or not, but I don't like you. Not one bit." He laughed. "And you find this funny why?"

"Because I know that you and Hudson are mates. And while you might say you don't like me, I know for a fact that we're going to be related soon. How soon, however, is not soon enough for Hudson. You have him on pins and needles."

"I don't give a shit how he spends his free time. And just because that is what we came up with as a problem, it doesn't mean that anything is going to happen between us. I have a job to do, and I'm going to do it." He laughed again. "How would you like to hear how a dragon laughs out of his ass? I could easily show you that. Or maybe how it feels to have his tongue wrapped around his tail. Either one would suit me just fine."

"You're very violent, aren't you? Well, that's not the only reason that I'm here. There is a faerie that belonged to the man too. I'd like for you to speak to him and find out what he knows." Winnie went to her office door and whistled. When the tiny man came out of the room and sat on her palm, she introduced them to each other. "Oh. I guess you heard about that as well."

"Believe it or not, I've done this before, without your help. Which, right now, is neither helpful nor very productive. Go away and leave me to my work. And keep your family away as well. There has been a revolving door of them here all day." He crossed his arms over his chest, she supposed in a display of manliness. "What do you want, damn it?"

"How are you doing in your work to keep my family

safe?" She asked him if any of them were hurt or dead. "No, but I don't think that has anything to do with what you're supposed to be doing. Does it?"

"Right now there are over a thousand faeries at the school where your sons are going. They are not only watching over them, but they are making sure that they're eating enough and doing their homework. One of them is even tutoring your youngest in his spelling. You might want to have a look at his scores and see how much he's improving." He said that he would. "Your mate is currently being watched over by a dozen of my men. There would be more, but she's in and out of so many places that I've had to stage them all over town so that they could watch her moving. She isn't taking this very seriously, so I have to."

"I'll talk to her about it. And my brothers? I'm assuming that you've set people on them as well." She said that she had. "Me as well?"

"No, not you. I haven't because I don't care for you. That's the way that I work so that I can't ever get paid." He frowned. "Of course there is someone watching over you at all times. Christ, do you think I'm stupid? There are enough brownies around you at any given time that we could cover the state with them, if they stood side by side. And that's not counting the pack members that are out there, as well as a couple of bears and a tiger. Have you even noticed that you have a different driver? Or that your gardener isn't working far from the house?"

"No, I've been distracted. And it's your fault that I am. For some reason, Hudson is coming to me about you instead of talking to you himself." She told Cooper that she'd barred him from coming near her. "Why is that? You know what will happen to him if he doesn't get to be with you now that you're found for him."

"I was never lost, you moron. And I told him if he wanted me to keep his family safe, he couldn't be coming around here distracting me. Like you have done." He laughed. "I don't know if anyone has told you this or not, but you're not all that funny, nor handsome. In fact, I think that—"

Someone was close, someone that she could feel his intent. Not all of it, but enough to know that he was with the slayers somehow and that he was sent for her. Waiting for him to move or something so that she could pinpoint where he was exactly, Winnie used her extra skills to search his mind. Then from there, someone that he reported to. This guy was nothing more than a front man, but he had caused some major problems.

"What is it?" Winnie told him to shut up. Surprisingly, he did. But when she moved toward the door to touch it, he was right behind her. The person out there wasn't friends with either of them, but he was going to give them a nice show. So, she decided, would she.

"Go to the office and stay there." He shook his head. "Look, dumbass. I have to deal with this, and if you're standing right here where you can be seen, the fucking slayer will know that you're aware of me. Go to the office. Barbed, make sure that he's quiet."

"My lord, I'd go if I were you. She's very capable of keeping herself out of harm's way, but won't if you are there too." He left, but he told her that he was there if she needed him. Barbed nodded once to her, and she knew that he understood what she was doing. The king would have his army before she could open the door.

The man standing there was indeed a slayer. He wasn't the one that she needed to kill, but close enough. Opening the door, she pulled her magic around her. It would not only cover the fact that she wasn't human, but it would also change her appearance. Winnie smiled as she stared at the man. She often wondered if it looked as tight as it felt on her face.

"Hello, ma'am. I'm with the Gazette. I'm here in your neighborhood to take a survey about what you'd like to see in our paper. May I come inside?" She told him that she had something on the stove and let a scent linger toward him. "Oh, that smells very good. Is it for the husband when he comes home?"

He tried to push his way into the house, but she knew that he wouldn't get far. The house, like her, was full of magic, and as soon as he stepped over the threshold, she shoved him against the wall with a knife to his throat.

"You picked the wrong house, dick." Winnie felt his fear and she smiled at him. She wanted to play, but instead let him see her for what she was. That was all it took for him to wet his pants and cry. "It's really too bad that you caught me on one of my good days. If you'd have been here yesterday, you'd already have your throat split and I'd be feasting on your liver." She wouldn't have, but he didn't have to know that.

"Don't kill me. They said that you were harmless, but a dragon lover." She licked his face and he whimpered. "I have a wife and two children."

"You have no one. Don't lie to me again. Who sent you here?" He told her that he couldn't tell her. "Then you will die now. I've no use for liars and people who are useless."

She pushed the blade of the knife into his throat and watched the small stream of blood run down his neck. He cried out like she'd stabbed him, but didn't speak again. The next time she asked him something, he'd tell her or die. It mattered little to her.

"The group that I belong to, we have men out all over town looking for dragon lovers. Once we've been invited into the house, we use magic on the people to make them tell us how they feel about dragons." He handed her the small vial when she told him to. "It's just something we slip into their tea or whatever they're drinking. It won't hurt anyone that has the same thoughts we do on dragons."

"So what do you think about them?" He told her what she had expected, death to the dragon. "Yeah, so how many have you seen? I'm assuming that someone that hates them, you have hurt one or two, or even killed off a couple. And in my way of thinking, once you've seen a dragon, magnificent creatures that they are, you can't help but think they're all cuddly and soft, right?"

"There aren't any. Dragons, I mean. They're just something that someone has made up, to scare young children into behaving. We have all heard the stories. Haven't you?" She nodded at him and waited. "I only joined this thing because it pays well. And I could use the money. I mean, who can't, right?"

"So, you're willing to drug some unsuspecting people and then report back to your boss, right? What's it to you whether or not they believe in them?" He shrugged and she dug the knife in a little deeper. "I don't want a half assed answer. If I did then I'd ask the man in the other room for one. He's about as stupid as they come, as far as I'm concerned."

"Nothing comes of it. I go back, give them my report of about half the people believing and the other half being followers, and go home. I get two hundred bucks for doing this shit for a few hours." She knew the moment that Cooper came out of the room. "You her husband? Your dinner sure smells good. But your wife here, she's got some major control issues, don't you think?"

"Yes, I've noticed that. And she's not my wife, but my bodyguard. You, young man, are so fucked right now." Winnie smiled at the kid and showed him her fangs. He didn't say anything, but looked at Cooper as he continued. "You're going to die, kid, if you don't watch your step. She's told me over and over, she doesn't play well with people."

Winnie raped his mind. There wasn't too much about what he was doing…he really was just making up surveys that he used. Drugging the people that he went to see, he would ransack their homes and take cash from them before walking out. The little shit was an entrepreneur at its best. Then Winnie reached beyond his mind to that of his boss.

"The people that you tell your boss about that believe in dragons are killed, did you know that? None of them are even aware that you were in their home; the drug you are giving them not only wipes out all memory of the conversation that you had with them, but also renders them unconscious until another group goes there, robs them of the stuff that you deemed unworthy, then murders them where you left them." He said no, that wasn't right. "Right or not, it's what happens. Thanks to you and your stupidity."

"I don't believe in this shit. How is it my fault?" Winnie looked at Cooper, then back at the man. "You can't be seriously believing any of this crap. I mean, who the fuck thinks there are dragons in the first place?"

"I do. He does as well. In fact, since I'm going to kill you anyway, I'm going to tell you who he is. This is Cooper Manning, king of all dragons. His father before him was king as well, but he died one night making his children safe." The man stared at Cooper. "And you know what? He's by far a better man than you would ever be. And I don't even like him. Cooper, show him your dragon."

Winnie felt it, the magic that was used to shift him into something that he was born to be. Cooper's breath burned at her back; not enough to hurt her, but to let her know that he was there. Then he rested his head on her shoulder, and she could see his body armor then. Cooper was ready for war... and then he breathed hard on the kid. Just like that, he fainted in her arms. Or died. It mattered little, so she let him fall to the floor and looked at the vial that he'd given her.

"I'm going to give this to him. I need for you to take him to a parking lot and leave him there. Hopefully someone will run over him and I won't have to deal with him." She pulled a little syringe from the air and stuck it into his underarm. "I'll know his every move now. And I'll clone his phone, too."

Winnie turned to Cooper, who was a glorious looking dragon. And when he stared at her, she knew that he thought that she actually was going to kill the man. Instead of telling him that she wasn't a murderer, she decided that it mattered little what she said to him. Winnie was a murderer, and she'd done it more often than not to someone that was out for him. While she was in her office, he shifted back to his old bastard self but stayed out of her way.

The phone was easy to take care of, and the small tracker she'd put on him was showing on her computer well. By the time Hudson and Lincoln showed up, she'd drugged the man and ruffed him up a little so that he'd think that he'd been robbed. When Lincoln and Cooper left with the man, Hudson was there at the door and she asked him what he wanted.

"I think we should talk, don't you?" Winnie told him she was too busy to shoot the shit with anyone, especially him. "Yes, well, I can help you then. Even if it's only to make you a meal or two. I'm...I bought a house, and I find that I don't want to do anything to it until you see it."

"Look, Hudson, I'm here to kill a man that is going to kill you for no other reason than he thinks it's his right. And in his pursuit of trying to find you, he's killing off other people, humans, to fund his operations." He nodded, and she wondered if he knew because of their connection, but thought it didn't matter. But she was concerned. "How much do you see in my head?"

"All that you'll let me." She nodded. "You've had a hard life, haven't you? I mean, your parents, they didn't give you much in the way of help or love."

"No. It's probably what made me what I am today." He asked her what that was. "You don't know? Cooper didn't tell you?"

"I didn't ask him. I suppose he would have if I wanted him to tell me, but I thought this was a conversation you and I should have." She asked him how much he really wanted to know. "Anything that you'll share with me. And so you know, I think that Xavier got less of whatever we got than I did."

"He did." Hudson nodded. "You really want to know it all? What I am? What sort of magic that we have? You want it all?"

"Yes." She nodded once and told him to stand still. "All right. Are you going to shift into something more?"

"Yes." She didn't know how much he'd be able to handle, but she didn't care to have a mate, and if they ran him off, then she'd be better for it. Winnie let herself go and let him see her.

"Mother fuck."

~~~

57

Hudson had a horrific need to run. Nothing could have prepared him for what stood before him. She was both terrifying and beautiful. After asking permission, he moved closer to her and put out his hand to touch the wings at her back.

"They're...I've never seen anything so beautiful in my life." She didn't speak, but watched him with the bluest eyes he'd ever seen. "Can you spread them out for me?"

When her wings opened up, he could see that he'd been wrong about one thing. They weren't just beautiful, but breathtakingly so. And when he got closer to her, he could see that they were covered in animal faces...wolves, dragons. There were faeries and brownies. A bear and a tiger were next to a puma and snake. He asked her what they meant.

"What you should ask is why, not what. I am everything." Hudson looked at her face and was startled by the change there too. She was covered in sigils that were, he'd bet, as old as time. "When the Dragon Board brought me before them, I thought it was to reward me for bringing them the dragon, but they gave me this. To find and fight them. I am all creatures, should I need them. I can switch to anything."

"How did you find the dragon?" She stretched out her wings again before tucking them behind her. "Christ, you're beautiful. Honestly, the word seems so little compared to how I see you."

"There were signs around our village. I didn't know what they said...I couldn't read, nor could I have read the words written on them. They were in dragon." Hudson nodded and watched as she shifted back to the Winnie he knew. He was both relieved and disappointed. "It took me several days to read what was there. The lettering was different than the signs I'd seen, so I played with them until one day, they just snapped into my head. I think that the Board knew something that I didn't at the time."

She moved to the window and looked out. He knew the view there…it was the back of another building. A garage, he thought. There were trash cans overflowing with garbage and other debris. When she didn't speak right away, he pulled a chair from the table and waited.

"The dragon had lost his mate. But instead of taking heed to the Board's warning about becoming a monster, he took it upon himself to kill humans. They were responsible for her death, you see." He told her that they were responsible for his mother's death as well. "If humans have no understanding for something, their first instinct is to kill it. I've never understood that about them."

"How long did it take you to find the dragon?" She told him only a few days. "That fast? You must have worked day and night to do that."

"I was starving. The money that I thought I'd get for his capture was going to feed me. And shelter me. My parents, they were no help to me. Not that they'd ever been, unless you count tossing me out on my ass when I was too young to survive, or beating me near to death when that suited them better. I left them then and I've not kept in contact with them in decades. I thought them to be dead." He told her he was sorry. "No reason to be. It wasn't your fault. But the dragon was taken to them and the Board, different members than there are now, decided that I would work for them. And they gave me this."

"Magic." She nodded and turned to him. "You can shift into anything, you said. Even a dragon? And if you can, are you able to fly?"

"Yes, to both. I can fly and use flames should I need to.

With the magic that they gave me was also instructions on how to become anything. The first week after they gave me this, I was down and out. When I woke, they told me what they'd done, how I was going to be rewarded, and who I would work for. Your father was my first client. Then after that, I served you all by keeping you safe. You were the first and last of your kind, did you know that?"

"We're dragons that were made to shift into humans. Most shifters are humans that can shift into their other self." Winnie nodded and said it was more than that. "Like what more? I mean, you know more than we do, I would imagine."

"Shifter dragons don't have tears that make gems. Well, that's not entirely true. They have them, but not on the scale that you guys have. I'm to understand that you can not only make them with different feelings, but they're larger and worth more." He said that he'd not known that. "You can't change a person either. Do you know why you are so special that you need someone like me to watch over you?"

"I never really thought about it." She didn't say anything, and he'd bet she was waiting on him to figure it out. "I don't know. I never knew that we were all that special, other than how we were changed."

"The witch that gave your father the spell that took his life, she used all her considerable magic to put it together. She was an earthen faerie, one that could use all the elements of the world to make her powerful. It's the reason, as first born, that Cooper can use those same elements. And all of you, to some degree. Her magic was white, as pure as the snow and as clean as the waterways that she used." Hudson held his breath. What she said next was going to change everything for him and his family, he knew it. "You are the earth, the air, and the water. The very breath that every being uses is

60

because of you and your family. The water that sustains them, it's because you are here. The earth that feeds them, it brings fruits and other things to their table because you are alive. Nothing in this world would be, nothing at all, if you were not a part of it."

"Why?" He thought that he knew the reason why, but he needed her to tell him. Hudson watched her face as she struggled, either to find him an answer or to put it into words that he could relate to. "Why are we so important to all of that?"

"Because you were created from it. The magic there, it was used to make you. So much of it was taken from the earth and the other elements that it would have died; the world as you know it would have ceased to exist had you not lived and become. Your father knew this. It was why he was so willing to give his life for you all to live. So that the world, and everything in it, would be able to survive. Because without you, before or after he gave it to you, the world would not have come to be. Nothing or none of us would have."

Hudson sat very still. It was a great deal. Not just the information, but the responsibility that was his and his brothers'. Never had he heard the story of this. And he doubted that any of his brothers had either. He looked up at her when she said his name. He knew something then that had never been a part of his thought process before. Knowledge that he never had before the truth of his life came to him.

"The book, it knows this?" She nodded, and told him that it did. "It's why we're needed. Not just a dragon, but our dragon needs to open it. And once it's opened, the magic within, it'll be more than anyone can handle. It'll destroy everything."

"Including you and your family, yes." Hudson nodded,

then stood up. He moved toward her, needing the contact of her skin to his more than ever. "Touching me will give you more, Hudson. Are you ready for that?"

"Yes, I need you." She said she understood. "Do you, Winnie? Do you really understand how much I need you? How hard it's been not to touch you?"

"Yes, I need you as well." Hudson ran his fingers over her shoulder, then her cheek. "Hudson, please, claim me."

Claim her. He had a feeling that it wasn't just words, but that he needed to claim her as his own. She'd not just be his mate, but his in all things. Kissing her, pulling her body to his, he looked into her eyes and noticed something that he'd not before. They were there.

The animals that she'd been, could be and would be again, were dancing behind her eyes. She was the all that she had told him, and so much more. And the words that he needed, the claiming ones that would bind them in ways that a simple mate to mate would not, came into his head.

"I, Hudson William Manning, second son of Cooper Manning, former king of all dragons, shifters and alike, claim you, Wendall, dragon protector, healer of worlds, as my own." Winnie was his...he felt their bond as it wrapped around them. "I love you with all my heart."

"And I you, but you should know something right now. I'm a very jealous person." He grinned, and felt like a world of weight had been lifted from his heart. "Take me, you big dummy. Then I have work to do."

Chapter 5

Ross wasn't sure what to think now. He'd had such plans, and the means to ensure that they came out the way he wanted them to. But the Manning dragons were not like anyone he'd ever seen before. Or had dealt with. They were... well, he hated to admit it, but they were brilliant. Not even hiding the fact that they were dragons, and this irritated him more than he could put into words. Everyone seemed to have their best interests at heart. He looked at the man, a child in comparison to him, again.

"I don't know what happened, if you're going to ask me again. I don't even know where I was, how I ended up robbed in the parking lot. And I haven't the slightest idea why I was arrested either. They have me on all sorts of counts of breaking and entering, and I'm not even sure what they're talking about." The kid—Ross hadn't ever bothered learning their names—glared at him. "You know anything about this?"

"You mean other than the police called me because you had my number in your phone? Or the fact that you asked for me when you woke from what they thought was a drunken stupor? No, I know nothing at all. Oh, I forgot, there were the drugs in your system that seem to have turned up in a lot of murders around the state. There is that." Ross wanted to pull a gun out and kill the fucker, but that would solve nothing. "The only reason that you're alive right now is because I'm pretty sure that the police are waiting for me to put a bullet in your head, and when they find your body, they'll come knocking at my door. And that is nothing that I want right now."

"My brother is still in jail. I thought you were going to be getting him out." Ross had to think what he was talking about. "They arrested him for trying to murder some guy, when all along he was aiming for his own wife. She's bad news. You said, and I quote, you'd be getting him out 'so we could tag team this thing you got me doing.'"

"Oh yes, the man who decided that he had something on the side, and it was better than he was getting at home. And let me remember the details of his woes. His wife had gotten big. With his child, no less, and he didn't care for it. Nor the time she was spending away from him while she held down a job to feed said child." The kid shook his head. "What is it I have wrong? I'm sure that whatever it is, it'll be profound."

"He said that she'd not let him have the card. The money card that gets filled up every month for food." Ross asked him if he wasn't being fed. "I suppose so. But Debbie was buying real food that had to be cooked, and not letting him trade the money in for stuff for him. I guess you can't buy beer and weed with that thing."

"No, you can't. Imagine that, the government telling someone that they can't get high or drunk on their dime." The kid nodded, as if that was something he couldn't believe either. "So this paragon of a brother of yours, what will he do once he gets out of jail? I'm assuming that he still wants that card?"

"Yeah, he does, but I think he's got something else planned for his woman. He didn't tell me what, but he said that as soon as he's out, which you said you'd help with, he was going to sell off the kid and deal with Debbie. It's the dealing with her part I don't know. I got a clue, but I don't think I'd want to be her when he gets out." Ross wondered if anyone did anything themselves for self-improvement. Or did they just suck the tit of the welfare offices and then expect they'd get more.

He knew that there were people out there, a great many of them, who were struggling to make it. And that the food card, or whatever it was, helped keep them from starving each month. This man and his family, however, thought that government ticket was just that for them. The lotto that somehow owed them. Ross just didn't understand people like this.

"I'm not going to let him out so that he can screw up my plans. Because as many times as I warned you not to tell anyone what you were doing, I'm sure you told him. Didn't you?" He explained that it was his brother. "Yes, and not only do you seem to share the same traits, but a single brain cell as well. Where his is right now is fine with me. One moron that I have to deal with at the moment is about all I can stand for now."

"All right, but he ain't going to like it. Just saying." Ross didn't bother telling him that he was lucky to have his brother in jail. It was where they were all going to end up if he didn't get a better grade of people working for him. "What do you need for me to do now? I know I messed up on being the best of going out for your surveying in that area, but I know you must have someplace for me to go."

"Yes, I do. But I've since changed my mind. I need for you to do some reconnaissance on a family for me." The kid looked confused. "I need for you to watch a family for me and take notes."

"Oh, yeah. I can do that. You shouldn't use such big words. I'm not dumb—smartest one in my family, even—but those words just muddy up the waters for me. All right?" Ross told him he'd remember that in the future. "Thanks. Where are they now? I mean, do you want me to find them too?"

Ross was reasonably sure that they not only knew where the kid lived and each place he'd stopped since he woke up, but might even know where he lived as well. The dumb fucker had led them right to him.

What happened to the time when you could not only get good people to work for you, but you had them over for dinner and shit? And knew, without a doubt, that they'd not tell a soul where they had been, and would even take the hit for you when the time came. That just wasn't around any longer. Those people, loyal ones, had all died out.

After sending him on his way, home to rest up, he'd told him, Ross sat down at his desk again and pulled out his notes. They were extensive too. He'd been working on this project of his for a great many years. Looking at the drawing of the book he needed, Ross thought about what he was going to gain in all this. As soon as he had the book and all its secrets, he was going to be rich beyond his wildest dreams, and have so much magic that he'd be able to conjure up whatever he couldn't get. That was going to be a great life. But, he had to find the book.

The house had been locked up when he'd returned. He couldn't get past the barrier, some sort of magic that had been put around the house. Even posing as one of the many workers there, he couldn't get into the house. He would have to either get someone else to go get it for him, if it was there, or he was going to have to kill the man that had purchased the house before he'd been able to. Ross wasn't sure how that had happened, but he wasn't happy about it. He did hope that the man's death would make the magic disappear. A lot of big *ifs*, he thought.

Sadly, Ross thought he'd been around enough magic that he could simply put a counter spell against it, but nothing he tried worked. He'd seen the little faeries there the second time he'd tried to get in, and figured that whoever had blocked him had an in with the mother of all magic. And that was something that he couldn't work around.

Ross had never believed that dragons were the ones that held all the magic. Not held, really, but kept it safe. Fat lot of good it had done them. As far as Ross could see, there were few of them left. They were, from his knowledge and experience with them, sort of stupid. But not the Mannings.

It had taken him a long time to figure out why they were superior to others. He didn't know just how they were better, but he knew they were. And once he figured that out, that they were not like the other dragons he'd encountered, he knew that they'd have to be the ones that broke the seal on the book. The legend had said that a dragon of great heart, to which he had assumed meant a big dragon, would be the one that opened the book. But now he knew it was not the heart size, but the quality of the man.

"Why must legends be so vague? Or all mystical?" He'd read one that was so thick with prose and colorful words that it had taken him the better part of a decade to get it figured out. And all it was, was for a spell to make one sleep. "Christ,

I hate wordy magic."

His was simple. When he wanted you dead, he snapped his fingers. If he wanted something to come to him, he put out his hand. There were others too…simple, right to the point magic. Again, he thought of the Manning dragons.

They were neither showy nor simple. According to what he'd been able to unearth about them, which wasn't a great deal, they were smart, wealthy, and all of them as good looking as the next. Also, and this burned his ass more than anything, they were very generous with his money.

"Well, it will be my money when I'm finished with them." He looked at the latest tax returns from the oldest. Cooper Manning donated more money in a month than Ross made each year. But never, it seemed to him, took any credit for it from the townspeople.

Hello, Ross. How's it hanging? He didn't know who the person was in his head, but he'd bet anything that it was that person that owned the house. *Nope. Not even close. You should know that once you had little Howie in your house, I got a good picture of a lot of things. Including the fact that you killed the person living there, and currently have them stashed in the shed out back. Good thing it's cold out, don't you think? Or you'd be stinking up the place about now.*

"Howie? Who the hell is that?" The voice told him it was the kid. Ross knew the kid had a tracker on him, but that didn't explain how this person was able to speak to him this way. Trackers, he knew, didn't do this. "You get out of my head right now. You've no business whatsoever stalking me."

You should take better care the next time you have someone in your offices. I mean, so far as I can tell, you didn't even do a small search on him. What were you thinking? He said that he wasn't afraid. *Aren't you? You should be. I should have warned you not to lie to me. I do hate a liar. But from now on tell me the truth, or I'll make you pay. And dearly for it.*

"Who is this?" The laughter was generic, just like the voice that was talking to him. "The very least you can do is give me something to call you."

You're just fine the way you are. Oh, I'm not saying that you've not heard of me. I mean, you'd have to be pretty dense not to have heard of Wendall, don't you think? Wendall. It took his befuddled mind a few seconds to latch onto that name. *Bingo. The slayer of slayers. I have other titles too. Ones that I think you're more familiar with. Protector of Magic. Slayer of Black Magic. Oh, and one that I'm sure you remember — you did coin the phrase yourself — was Hitman for the Dragons. Honestly, I never really cared for that one myself, but it went over well for the people that worked for you. Didn't it, Ross the Black?*

"That title isn't one that I care for either." The voice told him that they didn't care. "Who is this? You know a great deal about me, yet I know not even your name. What is it?"

Tsk, tsk, Ross the Black. I just told you my name. Don't you believe me? Ross told her that he didn't. *Oh, and using compulsion on me doesn't work, or haven't you been told that? I'm immune to magic from others. It's why I'm so fucking good at my job. But I will give you this, you've been around a lot longer than I would have hoped. Why hasn't a dragon burned you to a crisp? Or better yet, just crushed you under their foot? That's what my plans for you are. To order a dragon to crush you.* He said that wasn't possible. *Isn't it? You'd be surprised what sort of things I can do with my magic. Like this.*

The windows to his office were gone. Not just opened, but simply gone. The cold air coming in was vicious, and he saw his breath as he looked around. When the fireplace that was in the room abruptly roared to life, he was actually fearful that it would burn him out of the house. Or himself. It was then that he looked at his computer.

"What do you think you're doing?" The person was in his files. All of them were opening up, and then disappearing. "Get out of my personal things. I'll not have you going through things that don't concern you."

Everything about you now concerns me, Ross. Didn't you understand that? I'm going to find you and kill you. Just as soon as I figure out who you work for. He denied it, but the person only laughed. *I have your records. Bank, taxes, and anything else that I need. If you don't report to anyone else, then who is paying you a monthly fee of...? Oh my, that's a goodly sum of money, now isn't it? Who is paying you forty thousand dollars a month? And for what purpose, if you don't work for anyone?*

"I am my own boss. I work from home and make my own way. Nor do I report to anyone." He had to think of something quickly, and knew that he'd failed when whoever it was laughed again. "It's from an inheritance that I receive."

Inheritance? My word, whoever did you outlive that liked you enough to give you money each month? But I don't think that's what really is going on here, do you? I mean, you're not a very nice person. And, I think I warned you not to lie to me. That's the last time that I'll warn you. He felt his balls tighten at the way this person was talking to him. *Where is the money coming from that funds this little venture of yours? And what does this man think you're going to be able to deliver to him once it's done? And you'll notice that I said thinks, because there is no way in hell you're going to be giving him shit.*

Ross tried to think what to say to her. He had a feeling, a very good one, that she knew as much as he did about the man he'd been dealing with. A man that Ross had been afraid of until today. Now, right at this moment, he would gladly tell this man that there wasn't going to be a deal, and that the money that he'd been funding him with was all gone too, rather than face this unknown person.

"I don't know their name. Or, like you, if it is a male or female." She told him that she was a woman. "Your name, it implies that you're a man."

I think that you've been around long enough to know that nothing is as easy or as simple as it sounds. He could almost feel her anger then; it was a feeling that he'd not felt from her before. *You have been a naughty boy, haven't you? We'll have to make sure that you pay for that. When you're dead.*

The connection abruptly closed. He wasn't sure if she was coming for him or if she had only just cut him off. Either way, he decided that he needed to get the fuck out of there. As he was tossing his things into a suitcase, he started to laugh. And then he had to sit down so that the laughter didn't hurt anymore.

Run to where? his mind asked. She was in his fucking head. It mattered little where he hid, where he went; she had a direct connection to his thoughts and his schemes. Ross was fucked. After centuries of planning and plotting the death of the dragons, it had only taken a single woman to bring him down, and Ross had no doubt that she would, too.

~~~

The house seemed to be perfect for the man she was with. There were a great many appliances in the kitchen area—that she neither knew what to call them nor could use—that he seemed to be most proud of getting. There was a coffee machine…Winnie knew that one. But the rest, the bigger items, she didn't have the first clue. Other than brand names, she was lost.

"You don't like it? We can change whatever you wish."

71

She said that wasn't it. "Then what? Even if the house isn't something that you like, we can—"

After she was sure that he was finished talking, she removed her hand from his mouth. "I like this house. The kitchen isn't something that I'm familiar with. I don't eat much." He grinned at her and she smiled back. "I'm too old to figure these things out, too. I never had a use for them and never learned how to use them. I'm sorry."

"Don't be. We'll hire us a cook and a housekeeper, and neither of us will have to worry about it." He pulled her into his arms. "I was hoping we could maybe stay here tonight. I've had the bedroom set up. Last night was amazing."

"Because you had sex all night long." He pointed out that she had as well. "Yes, but I need sleep, which apparently you do not."

"I do, but you are such a lovely person to keep awake with." He was boyishly charming, and very good in bed. A contradiction, yes, but she loved him for it. "What's the matter?"

"The house is perfect. I swear to you. But this part of it, it's not in my realm of needs. When the Board gave me this...whatever it's called, they didn't think that being hungry when I was working would be a good thing. Yes, I can eat, but I don't need to. So, I never really had any kind of use for either restaurants or a kitchen." She grinned at him. "But, I have gotten a taste for a juicy hamburger and french fries. With everything on it. Pickles and tomatoes are my favorite."

"I love a good burger too." He picked her up and sat her on the counter. Then he stepped between her legs. "How about I make you scream for mercy again, and then I feed you? I've been known to make a mean burger and fries."

"Do you ever think of anything but sex?" He looked like

he was thinking about it, then told her no. "I didn't think so. But, if we're going to have sex in this room, it might become one of my favorite places. Are you all right with that?"

"Strip." She was naked before he was, her magic giving him what he wanted. Then when he was bare to her touch, she reached between them and wrapped her fingers around his thick cock. "I love it when you touch me. The way your body responds to mine. Christ, I'm going to come before you."

She watched his face as she fisted him. He was beautiful in his need. Hudson had his eyes closed, his body bent so that she could touch him. Even his skin seemed to glow with her touch. The way he looked right now, the look of pure pleasure on his face, made her want to make this last forever. But she had needs too, and hers weren't getting fulfilled as she played with him.

"I need you." She laid back on the counter after releasing him. "Fill me, Hudson. I want to feel you all the way to my heart."

He slammed forward and did just that. Even as he stilled, his body hard with his need, she didn't move either. She wanted to feel him there for a moment, and he understood. But when he moved then, holding steady by gripping the counter on either side of her, Winnie put her hands on his shoulders. Hudson then took her breast into his mouth.

The man could do wonders with his mouth. And as he suckled her, just the very tip of her breast, she cried out with the pleasure. Needing more, she rolled her hips forward and wrapped her legs around his. He paused and looked at her.

"I love you." She told him that she loved him as well, but he'd better do something. "Ah, so impatient, aren't you? How about if I do this?"

He moved. It was more than just a flexing of his hips, more

than him sliding into her. He filled her more than he had ever done before. And when he lifted her from the counter, she felt him deeper, his cock seemed thicker.

When he pressed her against the wall, his body a part of hers, she looked into his eyes and saw everything. His love for her, the way he needed her, and his happiness. Winnie had never, in all her life, made anyone happy.

He took her slowly then, watching her face, sliding in and out of her masterfully. Never in all her life had anyone made her feel this way during sex. Then it occurred to her; this wasn't sex, this was making love. Being tender instead of fulfilling a need. She dearly loved this man and all that he had evoked in her.

"Come for me, love. Come and let me fill you with all that I am." She told him that he already had. "Then come so that I might enjoy watching you in your pleasure."

Her body bowed back. She screamed out a release that made her see rainbows and birds. Before she was finished, she came again, letting everything inside of her go as she reached for and touched the sky with this man. And when he bit into her shoulder, tearing none too gently at her flesh, she came again, this time with darkness swirling around her until she simply blinked out.

"Are you all right?" He was still holding her, the wall pressed behind her. Nodding once, she grinned. "I can honestly say that I've never rendered a woman unconscious before. It's very good for my ego. As much as I'd like to try that again, I'd probably die. Happily, yes, but dead all the same."

Hudson sat her on the floor but didn't let her go. This was something else that she'd never had before…tenderness. And all that went with it. When his belly growled, she laughed. He just grinned bigger.

"I, however, need to fill my belly. And with all the sex I've been having with my favorite person, I seem to be burning more calories every day." He wiggled his brows at her. "How about I fix us both a fat burger with all the trimmings, some crispy fries that are totally bad for us, and have naked lunch?"

Winnie burst out laughing. If she did this every day for the rest of her days, laughing with Hudson, she thought that she'd be a better person. Also, he was right…sex did burn a lot of calories.

As he made them dinner, he talked about what he had going on. She'd not realized that he worked, and he told her that they all did. Some from home, but most of them went to a real job every day. Including Carson. Winnie was glad to hear that; it made them seem less snobbish, even though none of them were.

She worked in her office that he'd set up for her until he called her to eat. It wasn't like she was getting anywhere with the information that she'd gotten off Ross's computer, but she'd only just started. Someone, she knew, was funding the man, and she was going to find them before killing them both.

Chapter 6

Debbie listened to the men. Well, she tried to. There were too many of them first of all, all big men with large hands. She kept stealing glances at the woman that was with them, but she seemed just as big, and meaner than them. Not that she'd spoken a single word since they'd asked her to come into the office, but she still scared her. A great deal.

Suddenly a shrill noise made her jump, and Debbie realized that the woman had whistled. Not one of those girly kinds, but both fingers in her mouth and loud enough to make all six of the men in the room shut up. Debbie stood up to do just whatever it was she wanted.

"Get out of here." She thought for sure she was talking to her until the woman pointed to the chair. "Not you. Them. They need to get out of here so you can focus. And to let you know, I will never hurt you. I think you've been beat around enough, don't you?"

"Yes, but I'm afraid of you." The woman—she couldn't remember her name at the moment—nodded. "I'm sorry. I don't know you, do I?"

"It's all right. They're about too much for me too. I'm Winnie. I guess Winnie Manning now. I am the mate to Hudson, one of the big guys here." Debbie nodded. "Your son, he's safe; you know that, don't you?"

"Yes. They have...there are other people watching him that won't ever allow Robert to touch him. But they were talking about his brother, Howie. I forgot about him." Winnie said she wished that she could. Debbie laughed. "I know what you mean. Robert wasn't like he is now. Never once had he hit me before he started doing drugs. This is the fourth time that I've left him. Each time he literally drags me home and I have to try again. But he hurt Robbie the last time, and I finally got out, or so I thought."

"Yes, well, what they were trying to tell you and ask you about was that Howie is working for a very bad man. I say it like that so you don't freak out again." Debbie nodded, gripping tightly on the arms of the chair. "Are you going to freak out if I talk to you?"

"Yes." Winnie laughed and told her that was good. "Freaking out or just being honest? I don't want to freak out, but I've been through a lot. And now all of this. I love that they're all being so nice to me, but I'm not used to big men. I mean, they're really big men, aren't they?"

"They are. But something that you will never have to worry about from them is whether they're as kind hearted as they are big. And they'd never hurt a woman. Unless she was hurting others. But I do need for you to trust me, and not to be afraid of me." Debbie told her that it was hard. "Yes, I know that. But I'm trying really hard not to scare you."

"I think that's what is scaring me. You're not being yourself, are you?" Winnie said that she wasn't. "Please, be who you are. When you're trying to be...I can only assume nice about what you have to say…you're very tense. And that's making me tense too."

Winnie sat there for several seconds. Debbie could tell that she was trying to fight whatever control she had over herself, but then she just said "Fuck it" and shook her head. Debbie watched her transform from a beautiful woman to something more. No less beautiful, but nothing like she'd been before. There were no other words to describe how she looked now.

"Don't run." She said that she wouldn't and noticed the fangs. "Are you going to scream? If you do, then they're going to break down the door and come in here. And not as humans."

"Dragons." Winnie nodded. "I won't scream. I don't know what I'm going to do, but I won't scream. What are you?"

"Magical." Debbie thought that was a good word for it. She was just magical. "I take care that no one hurts the dragons. And anyone else that might be a part of them. That would include you and your son."

"Because of what you are. You can fight them better this way?" Winnie told her that she was capable of dealing with scum in either form, but this one was herself. "You're very beautiful. I mean, colorful too. I love it."

"I'm going to stand now. I want you to see me like this, just in case I have to be when you're around. I don't want you to be afraid of me. Not when it's important that you're not." Debbie stood up when she did. "I have wings as well. You may touch them should you want, but I will warn you that some magic will be yours. I don't know what…it's different for every person, but you'll get something. And I've let your son touch them as well. I might have asked you had I really thought of it, but his safety is important."

"Yes, it is. And my dad, his too. They're all I have in this world." Winnie told her that she had them as well. "I know, but you guys, you're not like us."

"No. We're nothing like anyone you've ever encountered before." Winnie turned her back to her and Debbie touched her fingers over the silky wings. They were nothing like she'd thought they'd be. For some reason she had thought of feathers, but they were like paintings on sheets of silk.

There were animals there, faces too. She wondered about them, but thought it rude to ask. But Winnie seemed to understand and explained what they were. Animals to call, she told her. Creatures and things she could and would become.

"There is more, too. I can pull things from my body. Weapons should I need them." A gun appeared in her hand, a knife in the other. When they disappeared, she sat down. "I don't want you to ever worry that someone isn't watching over the three of you. So, I've asked for some help. Someone to stay with you at all times. This is Gentleman Jack."

The little person came into the room and sat on the floor. He looked about as big as a toddler, but had gray hair and a beard to match. He winked at her and she smiled. Jack was a charmer, she'd bet anything on that.

"Howdy, miss. I'm to be your protector. I'm a might stronger than the faeries that are with your boy and daddy, so Winnie here asked for me." She nodded and asked him what he was. "Right to the point, I like that about you already. I'm a troll. Not one of the big ones, but one that does good for the lady."

"Lady?" Jack told her. "The lady of nature? There really is one? I mean, I don't mean to sound so stupid, but there really is a Mother Nature?"

"Yes, there surely is. She's a kind woman when it suits her. She don't like being blamed for all the weather that goes around. The lady, she has people working for her that does it, and sometimes…well, they'll have a bad day and take it out on their jobs. But that's when you get to see her at her best. Making something pretty out of all that nonsense."

"So you're going to be with me all the time. How does that work?" He disappeared and she looked at Winnie. "I don't understand. Have I offended him already?"

"I'm here. Just not where you can gander at me." His face appeared and she smiled at him. "I'm armed too. Not like my lady here, but I can keep you safe. But you have to listen to me when I tell you something."

"I will. I promise. I don't want to die." Jack nodded and appeared fully again. "I work at the plant now. I'm supervisor for it. Will you be there with me too?"

"All the time. Except when you're doing your private things. I'll just be close enough that you can holler for me, and I'll be there lickety split."

"Now, I need to ask you a few questions. Mostly about your brother-in-law, but they'll be related to your husband as well. Like, do you know who Howie works for?" Debbie didn't even know he had a job. "Okay. How about your husband. Does Robert have a job? A time when he seems to have more money than other times?"

"If he has money, he doesn't tell me. He's terrified that I'll want some of it. Like for food and rent. We don't pay much, hardly anything at all, but he thinks that we should be getting it for free, like his friends are." Winnie said she understood. "There was a time a couple of weeks ago when he had enough cash to get a gun. The one that he shot at me with. He said that Howie had given him a bunch until he was hired too. I don't know what happened after that. I left him a few days later."

"That helps. And did Howie say what this work might entail?" She started to shake her head again, feeling bad because she wasn't much help, when she remembered something. "Even if you don't think it's important, it might be."

"There was this tall guy. Skinny. To be honest, I thought he was a homosexual, because of the way that he walked and gestured. But Howie assured me that he wasn't. I don't know why it should matter, but he got all pissy about it." Winnie asked if she saw anything else. "Yes. He had on the strangest shoes. They were rubber, though not like those clogs that people wear, but rubber boots. Like he was going wading or something."

The look on Winnie's face made Debbie think that she'd hit on something important. But when Winnie asked her more questions, like where did she see him, was he with someone else, she let it go. The man wasn't anyone that she might have hung out with, Debbie thought. He was kinda weird.

"Anything else? Did you hear his voice? Something he might have said that struck you as odd?" Debbie pointed out that she'd been across the street from him. "Then how did you know that he was his boss?"

"Oh. Howie told me. Like, he pointed to the man and said that he was his money bags. I understood that to mean that he was his boss." Debbie wondered what that had to do with things, but it wasn't really her business if they were going to keep her and Robbie safe. "You might also want to know that he doesn't drive all that much. He's very caution when he does. Robert told me that. Said the man had never learned and that was funny. Even my grandma knew how to drive before she passed away."

"It might be that he never learned because cars weren't around when he was born." She'd never thought of that. But then, she'd not realized that there were things that could be older than that. "Thank you for your help, Debbie. If you think of anything else, all you need to do is think of me. We have a connection now."

Debbie started out the door and remembered that she'd touched her. Turning back, she could see the confusion on her face and nearly asked her about it, but instead inquired about the magic she might have gotten.

"You are protected now, more than you were before. If you were to cut yourself, you'd heal almost immediately. Larger wounds, like the one where you were shot, those will heal quicker too. Not as fast as a smaller one, but faster." She nodded and asked if she was all right. "I am. I was just thinking of the clues you gave me."

"I hope I was helpful." Winnie said that she was. "Thank you, Winnie. You're a very good person. I don't think you let many people see that, but you really are."

Debbie went back to her own office after assuring the men that she was all right. It occurred to her to tell Hudson that Winnie was upset, but she wasn't sure that it wasn't just as she said, that she was thinking. Jack followed her to her office, talking a mile a minute about nothing in particular. It was going to be a long week if he continued to talk all the time. But it was good company too.

~~~

Hudson let his dragon consume him. It was easier for him to search out things in this form than it was if he was his human counterpart. As he looked around the woods behind his home, he could see heat signatures of the other creatures in the area that he'd not been able to as a human. He looked

83

at Winnie when she said his name.

"Now, I want you to close your eyes and think about a certain creature. Not like their name, but them. Or even your brothers. Think of one of them." He said he was thinking of Tristan and he popped into his vision. "See him? Tell me what he's doing."

"He's taking a piss. Standing in his bathroom at the hotel. How am I seeing this?" She said it was part of her magic she'd given him. "And I can see anyone?"

"Anything. Like if you're missing something, keys or whatever, just close your eyes and think of it and you'll be able to see it. Sometimes you have to move back from the object to see where it is, like on a piece of wood. You might have to back your vision of it up to see that it's on the table." He asked her why he'd had to become a dragon to do that. "I needed to make sure that you can do it as either. I know you can as a person. But it's good to know that you can as a dragon as well. Okay, one more thing. The animals here. Focus on one of them. I don't care what it is, just see it and hold the image in your mind."

He did what she asked and saw the wolf sitting in the dense trees. He was sure it was a full-blooded wolf and not a shifter. Asking her if it mattered which, she said that it did and he felt strangely different. Hudson looked at Winnie and knew that something had changed.

"Okay, that works. You can shift into other animals. People too, I would imagine, but since I'm the only one out here, we'll have to—" He asked her how to be himself again. "The same way you do as a dragon."

Shifting from the wolf to himself was easier than he'd thought it would be. But he was still slightly messed up about being able to shift into something else. He asked her

84

for a moment and she nodded. That was another thing about Winnie he loved…she was compassionate about new things with others.

"I changed into a wolf." She told him that she'd seen it. "No, what I mean is, I changed into a wolf. Like, I was a wolf."

"Yeah, I got it. I was here. And for the record, you did a great job of it too. But, being a human isn't as easy. There are things you'd have to know about the person. How they walk, the way they might use their hands, also habits that people don't think about." He asked her what that might be. "Well, silly things really, but like, do they use their fork for certain food items or a spoon? Do they shut the door when they're using the bathroom or leave it open for the world to see? Those sort of small things will get you tripped up."

She explained other things that he might be able to do. Like he could now easily make himself invisible. That wasn't as hard as he'd thought it would be either. There were other things, things that he was sort of freaked out about but let her explain. They were out here so that he could be safer if he should need the magic they shared.

Hudson knew that she was distracted. While she didn't treat him any differently, she wasn't as happy as she had been before leaving for the plant today. Something had upset her, and he wanted to fix it for her. But for as many times as he'd asked her, it was that many times that she'd given him the same answer but different versions of it. She was thinking.

As they were walking back to the house, her being her usual quiet self, he asked her about the meeting today with Debbie after they'd left the room. He wasn't sure that she had heard him then she spoke.

"Her husband did a number on her. I think his buddies as well. She's too afraid of all of you guys. Of me too, I guess, but I think we've come to a solution to that. By the way, Jack told me that she cries a lot. Like when she puts her son to bed and no one is around." Hudson said he thought that was normal for someone that had been abused like her. "I've set her up with a couple of people to work with. One of them is a spousal abuse survivor, the other a reformed abuser. They can get her through this."

"How is this person a reformed abuser?" He lauded when she answered him. "Set him on the right path, did you? Well, that's good. I suppose it's better than prison for some. The fear of Winnie in them."

They were nearly to the house when she stopped and turned to him. He thought she was going to tell him about her problems, but instead she told him that she'd met his mom, and his dad.

"You did?" She nodded and sat on a deck chair after wiping off the snow. "I remember her a little. I wasn't young when she was killed, but it's been so long. She was beautiful. And her dragon was the same color as mine. That mossy green." He thought of her meeting Winnie and Carson and smiled. "She would have loved you two. And been so proud of you for putting us in our places."

"You can see her if you wish." He asked her how. "Well, you have your vision now, and can bring her to your present, just an image of her, where you can see her and remember."

"I don't know. The last memories I have of her was seeing her devastated body after the humans were finished. They carved her up, taking what they thought they could use and some that they couldn't. It was pretty horrific to me." He asked her when she'd met her. "I'd like to know only because she was such an important part of my life."

"You have to remember that she was only a dragon.

I could speak to her, like you can me now, but I was more headstrong than I am now." He tried to imagine that and couldn't. Hudson thought that Winnie was very headstrong now. "She was looking for food. I think that your little brother had been born by then. If not, I know that she was with Tristan. He'd wandered off from her and she was frantic with the need to find him. I found her in the water, where she thought he'd fallen in."

"That sounds like Tristan. When we were smaller, he was forever wandering off. I'm assuming that you helped her find him." Winnie said that he'd found them. "So he came back?"

"Yes. He'd seen something that caught his attention. I don't remember what it was now, but he had a mouthful of flowers for your mom. They were worse for wear, but she acted like he'd given her the finest piece of meat and had cuddled them to her heart like they were gold." He told her that was a nice story. "Yes. For decades after I heard of her death, I would think of that. And when I did, I'd go to her faerie garden and see her. And every time I went, the same kind of flowers were lying next to her garden."

"Tristan?" She said that's what she'd always assumed. "That's a lovely thing to tell me. I don't remember him ever mentioning that he'd been to her garden. Knowing that he visits her makes me realize that I don't go often enough."

"The faeries should bring her here, to this land for you. It wouldn't be difficult for them to do so. Your father too. He's close to where she is. They have the most beautiful gardens. Bigger than I have ever seen since and before." He was touched about it and decided to make a trip to see them soon. "I've been thinking about something that Debbie told me. That the man that was giving them money for this project was tall and slender. Other things as well, but that is odd, don't you think?

I mean, Ross is neither of those things. I think she's met the guy he works for."

"What have you found out in his records? You said it was in code." She said that it was and she was getting it narrowed down. "I figured you would. What about the book? Does he mention it at all?"

"Just that he has marked off all the places that it isn't. The house, the one that Xavier bought, it's a factor in this. I don't know how yet, but I know that there is where we'll find it." Hudson told her what Carson had said. "Yes, I've looked too and not found it, but I know that something or someone knows where it is and what it is, and is holding it."

"But not for Ross or anyone else that isn't a dragon." Winnie told him that she didn't believe so or they would have given it or sold it to them by now. "Yes, I suppose you're right. But if it's in the house, where is it?"

Entering the house, he could smell dinner cooking. Yesterday they'd hired a cook and a few staff. There wasn't really much in the way of need for the staff, but Cooper pointed out that it was appearances as well as money for the people working for them. They opted to eat in the kitchen rather than the dining room. It was still being worked on anyway.

The veggie soup was good, the homemade bread that was with it even better. He ate three bowls of it before he was served his dinner of steak and a large baked potato. Hudson had noticed that he didn't eat as much as he used to either, and figured it was because of Winnie. He glanced up at her when she asked Finny, the cook, for some juice.

"Of course, miss. I have orange, grape, and lemon. Which would you prefer?" Winnie asked for a glass of all three. "I can do that for you. If you'd like, I can have it around more, should you want it."

"Yes, I'd like that. In the winter months, juice is very important to us because of the lack of as much sun. Make sure that you please serve some to Hudson too." He nodded at her wink and drank down a glass of grape juice too. "The fresher it is, the better it is for us."

They finished eating, her about half of what he did, but they both declined dessert. He'd never been a big fan of sweets, and she told him that she didn't like them at all. Fresh fruit and cheese were more to her liking. Hudson asked Finny to bring them some into the offices later. They both had a lot of work to do.

He was looking over the contract he'd been given by Lucas when his phone rang. He knew it was going to be someone he wasn't related to, but the voice on the other end wasn't anyone that he recognized. Hudson interrupted the person three times before he simply hung up on them. They were selling new windows or something.

When the phone rang the second time, he waited for the person to start talking before he closed his eyes and reached for them. He could see them there, sitting at a large desk that was covered in paperwork. What it was he had no idea, but it had nothing to do with windows. Hudson was ready to hang up when he felt Winnie near him.

Look around. They won't know that you can see into their home. Tell me what you see. All of it. He told her about the desk and the paperwork that was on it. *You can concentrate on it and read what is there. Is it billing? Can you see a name on any of it?*

No. it's just...It looks like it's just words on a sheet of paper. There are red marks on it, like someone is doing edits on it. He moved closer, amazed that he could do this. *It's a dissertation, I think. Someone's homework. Could they just be a teacher that is selling windows on the side?*

89

Maybe. Tell me about the house, the room. What do you see there? Hudson moved around the room and realized that the caller was quiet. *Tell them you'll need more information.* He did so and the voice told him that he had it.

It was then that he noticed that the person was reading right from a script. That the computer in front of the person had all the words there that he was saying. He told Winnie that. She explained that was normal.

The room looks expensive. She asked him why he'd think that. *I'm not sure. There are paned windows on the door that lead out to a snow-covered deck. The trees are covered with it too.*

The same as here, I think. So we can assume but not rule out that this person might be close to us. He didn't understand what that had to do with a sales call, but figured she was testing him. *I'm not testing you. Go on, tell me.*

Okay. The panes in the glass are clean, like they're new. The walls are covered in paper, expensive looking. And felt. Like in an old-fashioned house. The desk is dark wood. Walnut or a dark cherry. A lamp sits on it. The shade is green, but glass, like you'd see in a library. He moved around the room, telling her what he was seeing and what he thought about it. Finally he was at the person again. *I can't see their face. It's there…I can see the chin, the hands, but the face is a blur. Why is that?*

I'm not sure. He looked at the room again, this time thinking about how it looked. He realized then why he'd thought it was expensive. Because it was that and more. *What is it, Hudson?*

The room is fake. It's a room, but the things that I'm seeing, they're not real, like its photographs from a catalog. That's why I can't see the pictures on the walls. The things on the computer too are fake. The words there, they aren't in sentence form, but a jumble of words and punctuation. Winnie told him to look at the desk again. *Yes, the paperwork is just that, papers. There is nothing written on them. The thing is set up to look like.... Whoever this is, they knew that I'd be able to see into this.*

"Not you, but me." He looked at her when he realized that the phone had gone dead some time ago. "You dealt with the caller, the person, by asking for something to be sent to you via the mail. When they told you that they'd rather come out, you told them that it wouldn't work. They hung up. Hudson, you didn't need the call once you were in the house with them."

"This wasn't a test, was it?" She shook her head and stood up to start pacing. Hudson wasn't sure what was going on or why the person had called here, but— "They were doing the same thing I was doing. Searching the house for clues."

"They might have been, but the moment I felt someone doing that, I blocked them. It's why they kept you on the phone for so long. They were trying to break through." He was afraid and looked around the room then. So many clues that would give them away. Family pictures. Names on magazines that were lying about. Even the mail that he'd picked up this morning was there, with names of companies that he owned. "You know who it is, don't you?"

"Yes." She didn't elaborate and he didn't ask. He knew that when she wanted to share it, she'd tell him. Right now he could feel her confusion and frustration. "The boys, Cooper's sons, they need to be brought to the house and kept there for the next few days. Tell Cooper that he and Carson need to be extra careful of their phones and the television they watch."

"I'll tell him. What about the others?" She said they would need to regroup and watch out, and travel in pairs when they left for town. "This person, they're coming for us, aren't they?"

91

She stopped and looked at him, then nodded. "They're coming for you guys and the book. Which he doesn't have. We have to find it. Without it, we're doomed. This person, he's not going to stop, not ever."

"Do I want to know who it is?" She told him not yet. "All right. When you're ready, tell me. We'll deal with this."

Hudson trusted her, but he was afraid for them all. After she settled down, he held her. It was all he could offer her at the moment.

Chapter 7

Howie hated not doing something. He was lazy, sure, but he needed to keep busy so that he was getting cash. And everyone knew that cash was what made the world go around.

When someone pounded on his door, he pulled his gun out and went to it. He was shocked as shit to find his brother on the other side. Pulling him into a big bear hug, he told him how glad he was that he'd gotten out.

"Yes, no shit. I was in my cell, just hanging. You know? Well, there ain't that much else to do. Anyways, I was hanging out and this here guy comes and tells me that I'm free to go. Just opened the door and we walked out." Howie told him that his boss had come through for them. "Yeah. Now I got to get to Debbie. She's gonna give me what I want or I'm gonna take it. I'm thinking it'll be taking, don't you?"

"Yes." Howie had been thinking about Debbie a lot. She was living in a fine house with her daddy and kid. Eating three square a day and acting like nothing was wrong. He told his brother what he'd seen. "She's got a car too. A really new one that ain't got a single dent in it nowheres. And snow tires too. Not retreads like I have."

"I heard that too. I'm glad to know that you've been watching over her for me. That dad of hers, he came to see me too. Told me that I was going away and that I'd not be bothering them again. Sure did fuck up his talking, didn't I?" Howie hugged his brother again. "Got some cash too. That sucker that let me out, he gave me over two hundred bucks like it was nothing. We'll have some fun while we plan this out."

"You got it. How about we order some pizzas and beer?" Robert was all for that and Howie called it in. They'd be eating fine in about thirty minutes. "You got any plans that you want to share with me? I'm sort of not working. I got a job still, but right now I'm resting up. Sort of fucked up a little by getting myself in trouble."

"You'll be all right. We'll roll Debbie for the card; you know they put some extra on it when you got a kid. We'll get us some weed and shit, then sell off the rest for cash. What about that job you said you'd have for me?" Howie explained that it was the one he had. "Well, we'll wait him out, and take care of Debbie and her old man while we do."

When the pizzas arrived, they had already gotten a plan worked out. Howie knew where Debbie lived and worked. He'd tried to get money out of her account at the bank, due to being Robert's brother, but they said without him being on the account they'd not let him have any. Robert said he'd take care of that too.

"She's gotten uppity, don't you think?" Howie told him that she'd always been that way. "Yeah, never noticed it before then. And when she's gone and that kid is with somebody else, Mary said I could come live with her. There'd be plenty of room for you too. She lives in one of the subsidized places where she don't pay any rent."

After polishing off three of the five pizzas they'd gotten, the two of them went to see Debbie's house. It was a big one too, he'd told his brother. As soon as they pulled into the parking lot across from her, Robert got out and looked it over. Howie stood by him, just watching.

"Ain't even an apartment either." Howie said that it wasn't. "And look at the fence there. Wouldn't keep a big dog out, would it?"

"There is a bigger fence in the back. Wooden and all. I can't see over it, but I could get a glimpse of some of the shit she has on the deck thing. A new grill, and some chairs with a table. I'm betting there is a swing set too. And probably a big pool." Robert told him it would fetch a good price. "I never thought of that. But if you don't care none, I'd like to live there. When she's gone, I mean. I could use me some nice digs."

"You do that. I'll give it to you. But I get first dibs on the furniture. She might be a cunt, but she sure had nice tastes when it came to shit to sit on." Howie remembered that about her too. "'Course, if there is a pool or some shit, then I might want to live here with you. I could lay around it in the hot months like a king of his castle. Yes sirree bob, this is gonna fetch me a pretty penny when she's gone."

There was movement in the house and Howie looked at Debbie with her dad. They were sitting down at a big table and eating. He loved that his belly was full for the first time in a little while, but whatever they were having, he'd love to be in there having it too. Pizza just didn't fill a man up like a nice pot roast with all the trimmings did. He asked Robert when they were going to hit her up.

"Tomorrow when she gets her skinny ass home from

work, we'll be there awaiting on her. Her daddy and that kid will make her mind me. You see if they don't." Howie believed him. "We'll have some fun too, maybe mess it up a bit before she comes home. Not too much; we'll be living there, you know, but we can have some fun."

They headed back to his shitty apartment and his brother took his bed. He supposed that it was all right for one night… he had been in prison and missed having a bed. But the lumpy assed couch was itchy, and it had a couple of springs in it that were as mean as a rattle snake. Howie could not wait to be in his own home.

He was up at dawn, not because he was an early riser but because the couch had given him fits all night. Howie figured he might as well get up and get going rather than lay there waiting for the next bite of the spring.

Robert didn't rise until noon, and seemed to be in a fantastic mood. By then Howie's had soured all the way to being bitter. Robert wasn't being nice about nothing and it was getting on his nerves. Finally, when he asked him for some coffee that didn't get mixed up in a cup with hot water, Howie turned around and slugged him. Howie realized his mistake even before his brother hit the floor.

"You mother fucker." It was a free for all after that, mostly for his brother to freely hit him. Howie had a slow to burn temper that usually nothing ever came of, but Robert held grudges. And never forgot, however slight it might have been, anything made against him. And he was a mean prick.

By the time the fight was over Howie had a bloody nose, and was sure that it was broken. His ear was bleeding and he couldn't breathe right. The hitch in his back made it painful to stand, sit, or even to take a deep breath. And coughing was painful enough that he was sick after it. But he did take some

96

comfort in the mess he'd made of Robert.

"You think this is funny? Now I gotta go out and have people seeing me look like I've been pussy whipped." He knew better than to comment. Or to make fun of him. The next fight might just kill him. "You're not to leave my side today so that people will know we had a tussle. And make sure you limp a lot. I won't have them thinking that you got the best of me either. Fucker."

They were headed to the house today, but made a stop at the hardware store first. He should have known that he'd be paying for everything. Robert didn't spend his own money when there was someone else to spend theirs, and he was making purchases like he had all the money in the world. Good thing that Howie had remembered to bring his stash of cards he'd gotten from the houses that he'd been to. Otherwise, they'd have been sitting on the sidewalk with nothing but an empty bag.

After loading it all in his car, Howie was still wondering what Robert had needed a shovel for, as well as enough rope to probably tie up half the neighborhood. They made their way on over to Debbie's. It was nearly time for her to be home from work, so they had to hurry in bringing the shit in. But almost as soon as they broke into the house, Howie knew something was off.

"They ain't here." Robert said he could see that. "You thinking that they went over to the park or something? That they'll be meeting up for dinner before coming home?"

"In the snow? Christ, you're the dumbest shit I've ever known." Howie had met some of Robert's friends, and he wasn't sure he was right. "They'll be home soon. We just gotta be ready for them. Debbie is probably out spending my money on shit we don't need."

But the moment that they walked into the living room to set up, Howie knew they were fucked. Not only that, but he was almost positive that Robert being let out early was the first part of this little get together. The woman sitting on his new couch just smiled.

"Hello, dumbasses. Have a seat." Robert moved toward her. He never got so much as his hand that was carrying the ax lifted before his head was down on the floor, with him screaming in pain. "Sit or join him." Howie sat.

"What the fuck are you doing in my house?" Howie had a feeling that Robert was working on getting himself, maybe even both of them, murdered. Right there. Telling him to shut up only turned his attention to him. "Shut the fuck up, Howie. These people are trespassing and they hit me in the head."

"You're a moron. Both of you are, but I'm thinking that you're the dumbest of the two of you." Howie felt good about that until the woman turned to him. "Not to say that you're not stupid too, but he's dumber than you are. At least today. My name is Winnie. And we're here to settle up a couple of things. Not to say that I'm not going to kill you both, but for now, you have points in your favor. Where does your boss, Ross, get his idiots that work for him?"

"You don't tell her a damned thing, Howie. She's nothing but a bitch that's thinking of horning in on our shit." Howie didn't care so long as she didn't hurt him. "She's nothing, I tell you. And she ain't gonna be able to hurt us no more once I get my wind in me again."

"You aren't nothing but wind. Shut the fuck up before I shut you up." Robert stood up, not without some effort too. When he stood over the woman, Howie had just a moment of unease. Then it was gone when she stood up. She wasn't all that tall, nor built. "You want to try and take me on, buddy?

I've not had any fun in a long time, and this might be just what I need."

"I'm going to kill you." Howie wanted him to leave her alone. She was mean, and he was sure she was gonna hurt them both before this was done. And Robert was making her hurry things up a bit. Then she moved.

Howie knew that at some point, if he lived long enough, someone would ask him about the knife. Or whatever it was that she'd used to cut his brothers head clean off. As he stared at the head and the body, all he could think about was that he should have shut up. And when the first burble of laughter spilled from his lips, the woman slapped him hard across the face. Howie was thrilled to death to feel his face still on his head when she sat back down. She asked him if he wanted to live.

"I do. I surely do. But I'm thinking that even if you were to kill me, like you did him, nobody would ever find our bodies. Even if there was someone out there that wanted to look."

"No one would care." He had figured that out right away. "You going to help me, or do I lay your body next to your brother's in a shallow unmarked grave?"

"I looked that up one time. I was wondering why they always say that. A shallow grave. I figured out the unmarked part pretty good, but the shallow part, it sort of got me to wondering." She asked him what he'd found. "That the person isn't gonna bury you deep so that the critters can find you and have a feast on your body. You gonna dig one deep for me if I help?"

"Yes." He hadn't the slightest idea why, but he believed her. "I want to make something very clear right now. You do right by me and I'll let you go. You leave Debbie and her family alone. Forever."

"I was gonna do that anyway after this." He looked down at Robert. He wasn't bleeding like he thought he should have, and Howie wondered on that. But then he saw that there were burn marks all around his neck, like something hot and sharp had cut him up. "You're pretty powerful, ain't you?"

"Yes." He nodded and told her whatever she wanted, it was hers. "Good. I'm glad that you've gotten smart. Now, tell me where Ross gets the people that work for him."

~~~

Foster moved around the house with the workers. None of them could see him, which he was glad for, but he was right proud of the things going on in his house. It was going to be a fine place once they were finished up with what they were doing. And he couldn't wait to hang out with the new owner.

As the men were locking up for the day, he sat down on the step and looked around. Foster had died right here in this house. He didn't remember the year anymore, but he had been sick for a powerful long time before it took him. His wife had died some years before he had, and he'd been all alone here. Well, not this house, but the one that had been built on the same land all those years ago.

Ford had never been much company. He'd lived here for a long time too. Not nearly as long as he had, but he'd been one of the many owners over the years. Foster had only showed himself to the younger man because he'd been lonely. Now he was all alone again but for the workers.

Just as he was ready to go on back to his basement, the only true part of his original home, he heard someone on the front stoop. Blending into the darkness, he waited to see who it was.

It was the new owner, and a couple more people. But

when the women came in, he was so happy to see one of them that he nearly showed himself. Foster waited, however. He wasn't sure that she was as friendly as she used to be. To him anyway.

"They're starting on the upper floors in the morning. The kitchen is about done too." The owner moved into that room, but the woman he knew stayed behind. Foster waited to see what she was about when she smiled. "You coming?"

The owner—he'd not caught his name yet—had come back for her. But Winnie told him— Xavier, she called him— he had company. As he moved to the door, she told him that he was there, in the house already.

"An intruder? Who let him in?" She laughed again and the man smiled. "Why is it I have a feeling that we're not talking about the same thing?"

"He's not. An intruder, I mean. I think he might have lived here at one time." The rest of the people came out of the kitchen and stood in the main hall with him. Winnie sure was a pretty thing, and nice as could be. "Everyone, I'd like you to meet Foster. Like me, he didn't have a last name, but he adopted Greens as his name. For the green grasses of the home that he wanted to call his own."

"They would have been, too, had I had me the money." She laughed as he made himself known to them all. "You sure are a sight for sore eyes, my dear. The world treating you all right now?"

"Hardly. You should meet the family that I've become mated to." She introduced them all to him, including her mate Hudson Manning. "I think you have something that belongs to them, don't you?"

"I don't know what you're talking about." He hadn't blushed since he'd been a teenager and more than likely

101

couldn't now, but he felt it, the heat of it on his old cheeks. "Ford, he'll come back for it."

"He's dead." Foster told her that it didn't matter to him, that he was too. "True, but you should know that these people are the Manning dragons."

He had to believe her, but it sure was hard to. The Manning dragons were the first of their kind. Probably the onlyest ones too. As he moved toward the one that held onto his mate like she was the most precious thing in the world, he looked him over. And saw what he'd never in all his day expected to see.

"A dragon. You're a dadburned dragon." He told him that they all were. "I'll be tickled pink. I haven't ever...You know, I heard about you all. All my life, I heard about the Mannings. Goodness gracious, you must be older than dirt by now."

"We're pretty old, yes, but I think that Winnie is a little older." Foster told Cooper it wasn't right to point out a woman's age. "I'm sorry. I've forgotten my manners. My mother would be appalled right now."

"Never knew her, I hate to say, but I did read about her. On the quiet." He could tell that they didn't know what he was talking about, but he was fine with that. He looked at Winnie. "You sure have made a name for yourself, my lady. What did I hear the other day? Oh yeah, you were the protector of all."

"Just the dragons. You know why we're here, don't you, Foster? I mean, you have the book, don't you?" He said that he did. "And you'll hand it over to the rightful owners?"

"I might, I might, but I don't think it would be remiss of me to ask for something in return, now would it? I mean, a man, even a dead one, he has needs, don't he?" If he'd had a heart beating, it'd be pounding about now. "I need something from the owner of this here house."

"Anything you wish, if it's within my powers, it will be yours." Foster looked at the man who had spoken. He was a fine man, and he could tell he was a man of worth too. "I'm Xavier. I purchased your home a few weeks ago. I'd be proud to help you out."

"I don't want much." Xavier told him that it was fine. "You play chess? You read? I don't mean on one of them things that lights up the house like a million candles either. I mean a good, solid book. You read them?"

"Yes, I love to read, and I don't own a reader. I have a computer, but nothing to read books on. I love the smell of them, the way that they feel when you open them for the first time. And the sound of the pages when I turn them." Foster nodded, his excitement making him a little dizzy. "You wish to read with me?"

"Can't. Never learned how. My missus, she was onto me about it, but there just wasn't any time. We didn't have us any kids. I wish we would have, but she was taken when she was but a young bride, and I just never had it in me to marry again." Xavier said he was sorry. "Me too. I guess she really weren't no young bride, not with us being married for nearly forty years, but to me, we only had a wee bit of time together."

"What can I do for you, Foster? As I said, anything you wish, I'll do it for you." He asked him if he was against having a house guest. "You mean you? No, you can stay here for as long as you'd like. So long as we come to some understandings on certain things."

"You mean when you're here with a lady friend." Xavier laughed and said that was it. "I don't cotton to you not being mated to them, but a man like you, he'd have needs. I don't care about none of that for you." Xavier told him that he had one too, a condition. "You thinking of giving me a time to get out? I'm all right with that."

"No, I was thinking more in the way of me reading to you at nights. And perhaps if we can figure it out, playing chess. I'm not very good at it, but I can hold my own." Foster thought that this was just too good to be true, and started for the book when Xavier spoke again. "Foster, I'd be honored to have you stay here with me. To keep the loneliness away. But when the children start to come, even the ones we have now, will that bother you much?"

"You mean you all have some kids?" About the time he got the words out of his mouth, the door opened and two boys walked in. They were good looking ones too. He blended into the darkness so as not to scare them on their first day there.

He should have known better. That Winnie, she called him out, and then like he was a real person with hands and stuff, the kids were introduced to him. The little one, his name was John, told him he was glad to meet him, and Simon said that he'd like his help on some history lessons. Foster, he felt better than he had in a coon's age, he did.

"My mom, she died too." He looked at Winnie when little John told him that. He had noticed that both boys had their own faerie, and he was glad for it. "You ever see her? If you do, will you tell her that I miss her so much?"

"I'll be on the lookout for her, you can bet on that." He and the boys walked to the basement of the house. It was time to turn over the book. "If she left you with the Mannings, I might not be able to see her, you know."

"Why not?" Simon helped him lift the book out of the chest he'd had to drag it to, and looked at him as he asked again. "I know that there are a lot of the dead around, but she's gone from us."

"Well, you know that you only hang around here if you

got something to do or there is a thing bothering you." He hoped they'd not ask him what it was, so he hurried to his information. "Your momma, she left you with the Mannings so that she could just go on in peace. I'm betting that she felt so good about that, she didn't have to hang around and make sure you were gonna be all right. She knew it all the way to her heart."

"That's true? That the dead go on when they finish up their business?" He nodded at John and smiled at him. "You must have some powerful unfinished stuff, don't you, Mr. Foster? I hope that someday you get it all worked out too. But if you want help with it, I'll be there for you. I want you to be here, but if you want to go with your wife, I'll help you."

The kid couldn't have touched his heart any more if he'd pulled open his chest and touched it with his fingers. Foster walked up the stairs feeling like he'd been given the greatest of gifts. A little boy who liked him, a family that he was prouder of than a speckled pup under a little red wagon, and a home to live in. *Yes*, Foster thought, *I'm going to be here for a long while.*

After he handed the book over, or Simon did, he watched the people talk about the house. And the goings on about it. Foster did wonder if they were gonna open the book up. It was their right, he guessed, but nobody mentioned it again, nor did they seem inclined to be curious about it. After they started to put on their coats and all, he was left standing with Winnie, and he decided to ask her about it.

"They've decided to put it away someplace safe and not to open it. You know as well as I that the magic within it will destroy this earth." He said that he'd heard it, but never believed it. "It's true. And you've done them a great service by keeping it safe all these years. You more than likely saved all their lives with it. I have a gift for you as well."

"You don't have to be doing that." She said that it was well within her power to do so, and that the Dragon Board had told her to do it. "You gonna make me go on, missy? I'm not ready yet. I have to tell you that."

"No. No one is going to make you move on." She touched her fingers to where his heart had been. "You're a good man, Foster, and your wife said that she never thought of you as anything but a hero."

"No." Winnie nodded and he sat down. "She hated me. It's why she died all those years ago. Because of me being what I was. A money grubbing bastard that didn't have any heart left for her."

"She loved you and you her." He nodded and sobbed. "She said that if you'd not done what you had, that the two of you would have frozen that first winter. And if that hadn't killed you both, then you would have starved. You did right by her, and she knew it."

"I never stole another thing. Tell her that for me, will you? Tell her that even when I was tempted, I never did. That book...I took it, yeah, but it was for goodness." Winnie said she knew that. "You gave me such a gift, girl. I don't know how I'll ever repay you for this. It's been hurting me for many years."

"That's not the gift, Foster." He asked her what she meant. "I only told you that because I knew you were hurting from not knowing. Your gift from the dragons is much bigger."

She left him then, laughing her fool head off without telling him a dagburn thing. He was going to have to figure it out, he supposed, and when he did, he was gonna have to tell her how long it had taken him.

Foster headed to the basement and looked into the little

bathroom that had been put in under the stairs. But he went back when he realized something. It took him a whole five minutes of staring before he realized what he was seeing.

"Woman, get yourself back here and explain yourself." He stared at his reflection, something that he'd not seen in more decades than he'd been alive. "She done went and made me whole again. That dagburn woman, she gave me life again."

Foster decided that the basement wasn't good enough for this old man, and made his way to the upper levels. He was gonna sleep in a real bed tonight, even if he had to use some of the tarps as blankets. He was about as happy as he'd ever been in his entire being. Now he had to think of a last name for himself.

Chapter 8

Ross was playing the waiting game now. He'd figured out there was no point in hiding from the woman, nor did he think that she'd just give up now that she had her book. Glancing down at the newspaper, he wondered not for the first time why Ford hadn't told him that it was there in the house. But that was all lost to him now. The book, it seemed, had found its way to the dragons, and he was shit out of luck. The phone ringing next to him went unanswered again.

"Not going to listen to that again." The woman had been bothering him nonstop since she'd gotten the book, asking him who his money man was, how he'd gotten the people that worked for him. And even why the book had meant so much to him. "Money. Pure and simple. The money man, as you're so fond of calling him, just wanted to see the fucking dragons, and now even that is not going to happen. Nor am I getting paid."

So here he sat, in a stolen house, waiting for someone, more than likely the police or the woman, to come and get him. Then he'd spend the rest of his days in jail, wishing for death. Being as depressed as he was, he wondered why he didn't just take the gun that was in his top drawer and end it. It would be quicker than what was in store for him.

"Hello, jerkwad." He looked up and there she was. The woman again. "I think you've seen the papers, haven't you? The book is all ours now, and you're not going to be able to get what you wanted from it. What was that, anyway? Doesn't matter. We got it all now."

"What does it matter now? You have want you wanted." She said that she only had part. "You want my blood too? Go ahead. I'm sick of waiting on something to happen."

"What did your boss tell you about the book and dragons?" Ross figured that he was going to be in trouble anyway, so told her what he'd wanted. "Just to see a dragon. That's all he wanted for giving you thousands of dollars every month? I don't buy that, do you?"

"Then why am I not arrested? Surely you've spoken to the police, and know that I instrumented all this to see your downfall." She laughed. "I don't think you're very nice. What you're doing right now is the same as beating a man when he's down."

"Oh, I'm sorry. And here I thought that was what you did and I was following in your footsteps. Forgive me." He did not like this bitch. "So, you're wondering why you've not been arrested. Well, that's because the person that is funding you is still out there. And while you don't know who it is, I do. And I want them to come after you."

"So he can kill me?" She said that his demise wouldn't bother her, no. "You're a cold heartless bitch. Has anyone ever pointed that out to you before?"

"You'd be surprised at how many have said that to me. But they never lived long enough after pointing it out to me

110

that I cared all that much." He could believe that. "I know a great deal about you, Ross the Black. Once I figured out your real name, it wasn't that hard to figure out the rest. Like, who would have thought that you were there when the Civil War started? I was really curious if you had anything to do with it, but you didn't. I'm glad…that might have changed up a lot of history books. And that you killed your first person when you were only seven. I suppose in your mind it was kill or be killed, but you and I both know that wasn't it. Your brother was just a little kid who wanted to hang out with his big brother. I wonder what he might have thought if he'd known what sort of person you actually were."

Ross remembered his little brother. He'd been responsible for him after his mother had died. And his dad, always a bastard, had decided that Ross was going to be nursemaid for him. But after a few days of that, Ross had convinced his brother that he needed a bath. So he took him out to the deepest part of the pond near their home and let him go.

"So what? You know my life history. Why don't you tell me about yours and we can see who is the baddest? I have news for you, bitch, I have done a lot of shit over the years." She said that she had too. "Oh, like what? Pulling wings off butterflies? Cheating on a test? Fuck, lady, you're a saint compared to me."

"Really? Let me recount some things for you, if you want to listen. When I was just a child, I found a dragon. He was a big fucker too. I hunted him down and then took his tongue. Dragons can't breathe fire without a tongue, did you know that? Anyway, after that, I was given enough power to hunt them all down. Even going so far as to help a few of them live a lot longer than they might have." Ross knew this about her. Wendall the Protector had a long list of deeds in her favor.

"And just for the record, I'm not going to go there all pissy and end your life for you. I can read your mind, remember?"

He'd hoped that he could piss her off enough that she'd do just that. He didn't want to go to jail, nor did he want the problem of a trial. There were too many skeletons in his closet. Hell, Ross figured that he could fill a couple of houses for what he'd been doing all these years.

"I know where you got your recruits too. That was something that I had a hard time figuring out. But after spending a few hours with your buddy Howie—you remember him—I got it worked out. He's singing your work to anyone that will listen to him." He had forgotten about that little shit. Or at least he'd tried to. "And in the event it comes up, you're going to be accused of letting his brother out too. Just walked into the jail house, unlocked his door, and he got away. Too bad that some citizen had to go and kill him before the trial, but you'll be blamed for that one as well."

"Sure, just pile it on. What do I have to lose at this point?" She laughed and he just sighed heavily. "Really, why am I still here? You've got what you wanted. The book and enough dirt on me to put me away. Why not have someone come and get me?"

"I told you. I'm waiting on the person who is paying you." Ross told her that he'd not come all this way for that. "Are you sure? I'm not. I look to see this person in a couple of days. Probably less."

"To what end?" She didn't answer him, so he decided to start telling her things that he'd done. Arrested and out of this place would be better than no one but his own company, just waiting on someone to come here and take him away. "Look, lady. I'm a bad guy. I shot Ford in the head when the information that he gave me was not useful."

"I know that, moron." He really was getting pissed about her calling him names. "You've also killed a couple of other people since him. The man that owned the house you're in. I've already had the police come for that body. And then there is the guy who had the nerve to ask you for identification when he came to check on the electric box. But, for now, that doesn't matter. I'm waiting with you."

"I don't understand you." She told him she was very complex. "A pain in the ass too. Come on, just let's get this over with."

"No." He stood up then. He thought perhaps it had been a long time since he had because his legs were wobbly and his head spun. Of course, he hadn't eaten much either, so he surmised that could have been it. He was broke, and food and drinks cost money. Instead of fleeing as he'd wanted to do, he'd been sitting in the house just waiting, like the moron that she'd called him.

Ross ignored her then. It was easy since she stopped talking to him. Wandering around the house, he looked at the crap that the man had collected. A lot of it, he supposed, was very old, but for the most part Ross didn't get spending money on shit that was as old as he was. He'd seen all this before, the *primitive* table and chairs. The old buckets that he'd had to carry for water. Even the old-fashioned water pump that sat on the counter without the benefit of water running to it. Morons, that's what he thought of humans.

Why have you given up, he asked himself? He had too. Ross hadn't showered in the last three days. He had on the same clothing, his pajamas that he'd slept in when the mood struck him. There were stains on his feet where he'd dropped something on the floor and wiped it up with his feet. Ross had given completely up when the book was out of his reach.

113

The phone was ringing when he entered the kitchen. Picking it up, he didn't say anything. Not that he had been when he answered this line, but he could hear breathing. When the voice on the other end started talking, he simply hung up. The automated calls were about all this line ever got.

Moving from the kitchen to the dining room, he watched the snow falling. It was getting deep now, about a foot, he guessed. Even if he wanted to run, he'd not get far. Ross neither knew how to drive in snow nor was he going to shovel the shit. A man had his dignity.

Laughing at himself, he saw the deer that had been out several times a day since he'd locked himself away. He'd never even gone hunting. Not for sport, anyway. His father had…it was the way they had meat on the table. But toward the end of his life, even that had stopped. His dad had gone over the deep end when both his new young wife and his son had died on the same day.

"That was a red-letter day for me." He'd been Duncan Ross then. Or old man Duncan's kid. Ross had been causing trouble for not just his family but the townspeople too for a long time before he'd killed not just his brother, but his stepmother too. Holly had fallen down and had her head crushed by a horse's hoof right before his little brother had been drowned.

"Took me a few tries too, just to get the horse to step on her." Ross laughed at his own folly. His stepmother had been nice, he'd supposed now, but she'd been there and he didn't like it. Then when his dad, in his grief, had asked him to bathe his brother, he'd just let him go down for the count. "Stupid moron kept calling for me to help him, too."

The phone ringing startled him out of his thoughts. This time it was his, from his office. He'd never liked phones but

114

they had their uses, he supposed. Like avoiding talking to someone when they were wanting something from you. Ross heard the voice as he entered the office.

"I wanted to see if you would mind me coming to visit for a few days. I would like to see, if they would agree, if I could see a dragon. I know that you said that your part has fallen through, but I have paid a great deal of money for the opportunity to see one, and perhaps I could persuade them to let me. It would be my dying wish, so to speak." He heard the small laughter. It was more of a bad cough that had a little bit of giggle in it. "I should tell you that I am in town. I couldn't wait, and now I find that I'm glad that I did come along early. Call me and we'll set this up."

Just what he needed…the old man in his way. Ross sat down at his desk and thought about his lot in life. He had been on top of the world…magic, more than he could have ever imagined, and a plan. A good plan. A foolproof one at that. Then a woman had gotten into his head and he was sitting here feeling sorry for himself.

"You've come a long way." He nodded at his comment. "To think that you were able to make men do what you wanted, when you wanted, and it didn't harm you in any way. Now look at you."

Ross was still trying to figure out what the woman had done to him. His magic had been depleted to almost nothing. He could conjure a few things with it, but not as he'd been able to before. There was also the added bad news that he thought he was aging.

Just yesterday morning he'd looked in the mirror as he'd walked past it and saw grey hair. Not a little either, but his head was covered in the stuff. Today when he'd seen it, his head resembled the snow-covered mountain beyond the house, and it was falling out. By tomorrow or the day after, he'd be as bald as his father had been before dying. It had occurred to him that he should be concerned how much longer he had before he was dust in his shoes.

The knock at his door went unanswered, as did the phone ringing in his office and the house. Life, he'd come to imagine it, was peeling away from him, and he was exhausted with it. Ross closed his eyes and took a nap. He'd been doing that a lot lately as well.

~~~

Hudson found Winnie in her office. She was asleep at her desk again; this was the third morning in a row that he'd found her there. He wasn't worried about her getting harmed, but he was concerned about how restless she was, and pale. Picking her up, he smiled back when she looked at him and smiled. He kissed her on the nose and asked her if she wanted a shower with him.

"You've already had one." He grinned and wiggled his brows at her. "Oh, so you need me to come up and wash your back? I can do that, but I want the same from you."

"I'll wash every part of you, my love. And while I'm at it, I'll inspect you very closely so that I didn't miss an inch of you." He moved to the staircase as he continued. "I also have it on good authority that breakfast for you will be ready when you wake up from the much-needed nap you're going to take when I've finished with you."

"I don't want you to be finished with me." He said he could arrange that too. "Oh, Hudson, whatever am I going to do with you? You're so good to me. I love you."

"And I love you." Sitting her on the counter in their bathroom, he pulled her shirt up and over her head. Then he pulled off her baggy pants and socks. He laughed when he realized they were a pair of his and that she'd taken them from him. "I'll have to make sure you have cozy socks from now on."

When she was free of her outer clothing, he took his time in removing the rest. Tasting her flesh was a pastime that he could easily have done for weeks. Kissing her throat, tasting the heat of her, he moaned when she put her hand on his shoulder.

"Don't rush me, love. I need this as much as you do." Winnie nodded and let her hand drop into her lap. Looking at her, seeing her need written all over her face, he wasn't sure that he could take his time. So instead of touching her again with his mouth, he used his hands to feel the curve of her muscles in her back and legs.

He massaged her feet, one at a time, stretching her toes until they popped. Rubbing her ankles until she moaned. There was so much that he could do to her, and he was going to try his best to touch every part of her, just as he had threatened.

The backs of her legs were tight. He noticed the tiny scar on her knee. There was a small mark on her thigh, another on her hip. As he inspected each of these, he left a small kiss on them before moving on.

Winnie had a lovely belly button, which he suckled on and felt her move toward him. The bra she had on didn't mask the tightness of her nipples, the way her breasts had swelled. Even the dampness of her panties was enough of a turn on that he wanted to explore that more. But this was for her.

When the water turned on, he looked at her. She shrugged but didn't say anything. He knew that there were things she could do that they'd not explored, and wrote this off as one more of them. Removing her bra, he stood her up and turned her so that she faced the mirror. Cupping her breasts in his hands, he was excited about the way her pale breasts filled his darker hands.

"You're so beautiful." If she said anything, he didn't hear her. Or perhaps he'd been too focused on her. Leaning her over the sink, he ripped her panties off her body and took them to his nose. "I could come right now. Smelling you on these, it's like having a little slice of heaven."

He was naked too, his own power doing that quickly for him. Sliding into her hot pussy, he groaned at the heat, the tightness of it, and how she rippled around him. When he leaned over her, his hands running up and down her body, he watched her face in the mirror.

Taking her hard was what they both needed. When she held onto the counter, he held onto her. Fucking her hard, much harder than he'd meant to, he continued to watch her. And when she screamed out her release, he could have died right then and there. She was beyond beautiful; he wasn't sure there was a word that would describe it.

"Come, damn it. I need it."

He laughed and leaned over her. Biting into her shoulder, he let himself go. Her scream this time was so loud that the glass over them shattered. He pulled her back just as he came a second time. Then he held her.

"Christ, you nearly killed us both." He held her then, cradled her in his arms as he took her into the stall. Standing her on her feet, he noticed that they were both wobbly and a little shaky. "Lean on me and I'll wash your hair."

"I don't have the strength." He held her up, just barely, as he lathered up her hair, then her body. She was slippery and soft, but he managed to keep them both upright. After drying her off, he put her to bed and laid down beside her. Not to sleep — he had two meetings today that he couldn't miss — but to watch her sleep. She never stirred when he stood up and dressed. Leaving her a note, telling her that he'd be back for dinner, he slipped out of their bedroom and down the stairs. He was surprised to find Foster there.

"I have a favor to ask of the missus." Hudson told the elderly man that she was sleeping. "Yes, I noticed the light burning late last night. I'm not sleeping so well myself. I'd like to know if I could get me a job."

"Why would you think you'd need to ask her that? And you can do whatever you wish, Foster." He nodded, but didn't look so sure. "Why don't you tell me what has you upset and we can work from there?"

"How long I got?" He asked him what he meant. "You know. I was an old man when I died, and now I'm back to being among the living. I just want to know if my time is counting down or do I have only a little time."

"You're an immortal." He nodded, then looked at him with wide eyes. "The Board said that since you were so helpful to them, that they'd give you the gift of life. Winnie and I asked for it to be forever, with us, so that you could be a grandfather to the children."

"You did that? For me?" He said that they had. "Well, I'll be dogged gone. An immortal, huh? What kind of things do I gotta watch out for? You know, what can take it away from me?"

"Being beheaded." Foster told him he wasn't planning on that. "Also, a direct hit to the heart. That is a biggie. And you could be poisoned. Though only a few things can do that."

"Okay, that helps. I don't get myself shot in the heart — which hear tell, I never had one — and don't be making sword holding men mad at me. I'm guessing I should include women folk too. They're a might testy sometimes." Hudson asked him if he'd eaten. "I have, but I could always have me another meal. I've been without for a long time. That brother of yours, he got me a milkshake last night. Best thing I ever eat. And a fry. Who would have thought a tater could be that good?"

"I know. I love them as well." They entered the kitchen and Finny was just pulling biscuits out of the oven.

When Foster asked if he could have a couple, she told him to have a seat. Almost as soon as the two of them were seated, she put a platter of food in front of them. "What kind of job are you looking for, Foster?"

"You looking to raise cattle again?" Foster told Finny that he'd not rightly decided. "You go on over to my son's house. He's got him some cows that he's having trouble with. I remember hearing that you were a good man for that sort of stuff. You should be the county vet or something."

As the two of them talked about what it was he wanted to do, Hudson ate his breakfast and tried to decide how to get downtown. He loved to drive, but he wasn't all that good in the snow. As he sat there, Finny asked him if he was gonna take care of the driveway.

"How?" She told him. "That's brilliant, Finny. I have never thought of blowing my flame over the drive to get rid of the snow. I bet the rest of them haven't either. I love it."

He was going to do it too. As soon as he was done. And he wasn't going to tell his brothers either. They could figure it out on their own. Hudson was going to have the nicest and cleanest driveway in the state.

Kissing her on the cheek, he went out and tried it out on the places closest to the yard, that way if it got out of hand or didn't work, he'd not have to look at it all the time. But it did, much to the amusement of Foster. He felt so good about it that he took the old man to Finny's son on his way in. Hudson was in a fantastic mood after that.

The first meeting that he'd had set up was canceled due to weather. The second was still hours away. After opening up his computer to his work programs, he began working. The meeting today would take a lot of pressure off the warehouse they'd bought a few months ago. He'd found a person that wanted to use it, and they were going to pay rent. Not that they needed the money, not at all, but with the deal that he was hoping for, they'd be able to employ about three dozen people. Not a lot, but it was a beginning. Hudson had even looked into the other two buildings that he owned in the downtown area, and tried to figure out what could be done with them to generate more work.

He was deep into looking into a grocery store when Lincoln asked him if he had a minute.

"Anytime." Lincoln launched into his questions. He had two things going, and one that he wanted a partner on. "You asking me to partner with you or just looking?"

"You. I have an idea about opening up that greenhouse we were talking about. You remember. A few months ago we were talking about how we have to go all the way to the next town to get plants for the downtown planter?" He said he remembered. "Well, there is this building that could be converted to a greenhouse and market for the locals. Sort of a monthly way for them to sell off some of their extra produce and stuff, and have a place downtown that we could go to. I saw one in Cincinnati a few months ago and people love it."

"I like that idea. And what about the winter months? I mean, like right now." He told him how the place was enclosed too, that there were butchers as well as restaurants inside year-round. "Do you know how to get it started? I don't."

"I've been looking into that. Foster said at dinner the other night that he had a stand when he and his missus had too much. I don't mean him to run it—it's going to be big, I hope—but he could help us out. The man that runs the one in Cincy said he'd come up and help us plan it out. I think we should do it."

By the time his next meeting was ready, they'd worked out a schedule for the crew to go in and start on the renovations. There was also a list of people they could contact about the restaurants, as well as the meat market. Hudson went to his meeting with Lincoln alongside of him, with a whole new set of things to take care of. But he was thrilled beyond words that the city was going to benefit from this one.

Sitting down, he explained to the client what his plans were for the project, and he was all in too. It seemed that he had extra produce every month that he could sell cheap because it wasn't for the stores, and make a little profit off it instead of tossing it out. All in all, it was a pretty profitable and exciting morning. And it was only just after noon.

Chapter 9

Kirk looked at the contraption that he hated most of all. The telephone. Whoever had invented it needed to be shot. You couldn't see the person you were speaking to, nor could you hit them when they didn't give you the answers that you wanted to hear. It was a product of too much time on someone's hands, and he'd love to get ahold of them and tell them what a ruination of the world it was. And the cell phone…Well, he didn't want to get started on that.

"Did you hear from him?" He shook his head at his lovely wife. "I thought for sure this was in the bag. That is what he told us, wasn't it?"

"It'll be fine, I promise you. He might not be answering his phone simply because it's turned off or something. I know that can happen." Kirk refused to touch the cell phone that his wife carried, not even to look things up on it like she did all the time. "What does that thing you have say?"

"I've told you, you're not going to get me to look things up for you when you're perfectly capable of doing it on your own. I showed you how." And she had, several hundred

123

times. Mildred was very good with the thing. "What else have you learned? You look like you've been busy."

"Yes, she's here. I saw her yesterday." Mildred asked him where he'd seen her. "Just walking around. I thought she was with some kid, but it turns out that she was only on the sidewalk when he was. As far as I can tell, she has nothing to do with the Mannings. Are you sure about this?"

"Yes, I'm positive. What about the other two women you thought were her? Are you sure this one is her?" He said he was reasonably sure. "I guess that we'll have to figure that is about as close as we can do, then. I wish we had a picture of her."

Yes, that would have been most helpful. He had tried it a few times, getting a snapshot of the woman, but there was always something wrong with them when he tried to review them. Of course, his camera was as old as the building that he'd had to take the film to, but he refused to use anything else. Mildred had suggested, again, for him to take her cellphone, but he refused even that.

"There are two of them living on the estate, correct? Do you know which one of them is her?" He said that he was sure it was the darker haired one. "I cannot believe that we're this close to getting her, and we can't even figure out which woman she is. The ruse about the dragons and seeing one was working too. Now we have nothing."

"Not true. We do have a location now. And we do know that the dragons are here too. That is more than we had before." She said that was true. "The book...that is a mystery now. Even knowing that it's in this town was more than we had before. You have to be more positive, darling. It's not good to be so stressed out all the time. You should have a hobby, as I do."

He loved his hobby, as he called it. Beating people. Women mostly, but he loved to use his fists on them and pummel them to death. The blood and the sound of the breaking bones made him feel like he could sleep for a week afterwards. Kirk had taken the two women that he'd known weren't the women just to have some fun. But Mildred, she frowned on him doing it in a town they were in, so he'd taken them to the next town over. Still, it was his form of relaxation.

"I know that, but we've been doing this for so long, Kirk. I just want it done so we can move on with our lives. And now that that man has quit us, I'm just worried it's all been for nothing." He doubted very much they'd move on from anything. It was like them, a need to be into something. Like this project of finding the dragon queen. She was there, and once they found her, the others would fall into place behind her. "What are we doing this evening? I'm betting there isn't much in the way of places for us to eat, is there?"

"Not too much. But we'll be able to travel again once this is completed." The book was something that they'd heard of first from Raymond Ford, then his killer Ross. And now it had become an obsession with them. "What do you suppose the magic will mean to us? We have a great deal of it now."

"I don't care, do you?" He said no. It was the chase and the capture that they enjoyed. And spending money to get it. Their wealth was without end now. Smiling, he thought of just how they'd gotten to be so wealthy.

This was their third adventure this year. And it was only February. They'd do this for months at a time, go after something that was, to others, unattainable, and then bask in the knowledge that they'd done something that no other had. Like their life.

He and his wife had been around for so long that they'd

seen the first high-rise, car, and even ship. They had been there for the first light that lit up the houses, theirs included, as well as flying on planes. They were adventures for them. But there had been a time when they were thought of as horrible people. Kirk supposed, in a way, they still were.

"When this is done, what shall we do with Ross? I mean, he's not seen us, thanks to your plan of taking turns going to see him with hoods and masks. But he will have to be disposed of. I so would like to have a little fun with him first." Madeline said that he could should he want. "I've not been able to tear into someone here, as yet. Cameras you know, they're a destruction of all sorts of fun we used to have."

"I agree. But without them, the advancement of so much, we'd still be stuck in that one room shack waiting on someone to come and take care of us." He nodded. Their daughter had left them to their own devices, and he'd never forgiven her for that. "Once this is done, I'd very much like to go abroad for a few months. Give this hunt and kill thing a little rest."

It was the same every time. They'd say they were going to rest and relax, but they seldom did. For a few weeks, perhaps, but in the end, it was the fun they had that kept them alive. He was thinking about cash when she mentioned it as well.

"We'll have to go to the cave soon." He told her he thought tonight would be good. "All right. You go and I'll wait here. I don't like the dampness of it. And make sure that you bring me back a pretty too. I have a need for something spectacular made for me."

At dusk he drove himself to the cave. It took him most of the night to drive there, then an hour to climb the hill. It was why he was in such good shape…he'd been doing this for a very long time. Entering the deep cave they'd found decades ago, he was careful not to touch the walls. They were slimy, and made him think of worms…something to this day he could not stand to have touch him.

A dragon had been here for a while, spilling her riches for them. And when they found another cave or something that held treasures, they put it in here as well. The dragon, a large and cumbersome thing, had died, broken hearted he believed. They'd been afraid that they'd have to resort to other means of getting cash, but over the years it had been easy for them to take what they wanted, and usually, it was a great deal. They'd done all they had wanted, he guessed in the beginning to become rich. Now they did it simply because they could.

Kirk opened his satchel just as he was pushing the large boulder out of the way. The flashlight was in his mouth, so he wasn't sure what would have happened had he not had it shining on the large rock. Pulling the note away that had been stuck to the rock, he had to move into the room before he could read it. Kirk had to work on each word at a time, as his reading skills were not that good.

"Tank…. No, thank." He figured the next word was *you*. Which started with a *y* and that was just silly. "Thank you for the…I don't know. Thank you for something."

He put the flashlight in his other hand and pulled out his bag. He didn't have time for this nonsense, and hated that someone had come down here. Especially in the winter months. There weren't any footprints leading up to the place, so he had— Kirk looked around, waving his light over the area four times before he just sat down.

"It's gone." He glanced at the note that was still in his hand, and knew the person had thanked him for his money. "What are we to do? Where is our stuff?"

Getting up, he walked around the empty cave. There

had been so much in here the last time he'd come that he'd marveled if they'd have time to spend it all in several lifetimes. The chest that they'd found was laying on its side, the jewels that had been in it were nowhere to be seen. Even the chains that they'd once held a dragon with were gone, pulled from the wall and leaving gaping holes in it.

For the first time since their creation, he wished that he had a cell phone to call his wife. And to take some pictures. He was sure that she'd never believe him. That until she was here herself, she'd think he was pulling a joke on her. Not that he did that often, but she'd not believe it any more than he did right now.

Kirk walked around the area, about the size of two of those fields they chased an oval ball around on, and searched everywhere. He had no idea what he hoped to find...the person who had taken his things? A small map to where they had taken it all? But he found nothing, not even a chip of gold hidden around. He sat down with the missive still in his hand.

The note was going to be helpful. He didn't know if the person had signed it or not, but even if they hadn't, Mildred would be able to find out who it was. Robbed. They'd been robbed, and his head just couldn't seem to wrap around that.

Heading back to the hotel where they were staying, he didn't stop this time. Twice now he'd turned around and gone back to the cave and looked again. He'd even retraced his steps, thinking that he'd been in the wrong place. But it was accurate, and it was empty.

"Whatever is Mildred going to say to me?" He had actually thought that she might have been funning with him. But she wasn't the type to be joking about anything, and certainly not money. He had to pull over then, his belly and his head sick with this. Whatever were they going to do now?

"What is it?" He sat down on the little couch that had come with their room and Mildred came to him. "You have to tell me, Kirk. What's happened? Did you have an accident? Did you — ?"

"It's all gone." She asked him what. "The money, the jewels, it's all gone." He handed her the note, careful not to smudge it more. "This was on the stone when I got there. I didn't get it at first, so I wasn't sure what it meant. But I think they're thanking us for our money. How could they do that? It's not theirs."

"Thank you for the money. Sincerely, H. Who the heck is this *H* person?" He said he didn't know, he'd not gotten that far. "I swear to you, Kirk, if you have made a joke about this I'm not — "

"No, I swear to you. I'm not joking you. The place looks like they took a sweeper around the whole area and cleaned up. The chains on the walls? They're gone too. What would they want with them?" She said she was sure she didn't know. "Honey, we don't have any money. Not even enough to have us a vacation after this is done."

"We don't have enough for anything right now. Not until we get our funds back. Who knew it was there? I haven't told anyone, have you?" He swore that he'd not. "Then who? You go in the middle of the night. That way you can see cars following you. You're being careful, aren't you? What am I saying? Of course, you are. Why did they do this to us, Kirk?"

"I don't know. And to be so nice to leave us a note." Although, he was pretty sure that it wasn't to be nice, but to make them mad. "I think we should write down everyone we know that has their name start with a H. That way we can narrow it down."

"I think we both only know one person, and they're

129

dead." He was sure it couldn't have been them anyway. "What do we do? I know that I keep asking that, but really, Kirk, what are we to do? We can't even afford this place now. Not without money to fall back on. And trying to find another dragon will be nearly impossible this time. I mean, we know of the Manning dragons, but I doubt very much they'd be easy to lure into a cave, let us drug them, then chain them up."

"They took the chains." She glared at him. "I'm only trying to be practical. Those were very expensive and hard to come by. We had them made, if I remember. I doubt anyone would be willing to make them for us now, not without any funds."

"And we can't even promise them later, after we have a dragon. No one believes in them anymore. And had you asked me before this, I would have said they were all dead anyway. We did work very hard in keeping them when we found them, remember? This is messing up our plans." She stomped her foot. "I don't like to have plans messed with. You know that."

"I know, dear, I know that." He let her pace, something that she did better than anyone he knew. Kirk nearly suggested they go out to dinner and think on things, but she'd say no. They had no money. Mildred was the one that made such decisions for them. Kirk prided himself on being a planner, but she was the one that made it work. They were good together like that.

He thought of what they should do. Mildred would be in a better mood when there was a plan in place. He would as well.

"First thing tomorrow, I think we should set up a meeting with the dragons." She stopped pacing and told him to go on. "Then we try and gauge how they are going to react to our wanting to see one of them. I know that this it out there, but we can use the ploy that it's our dying wish. Which one of us is on the deathbed could be decided later. But if they let us see their dragon, then we can figure out what we need to capture the queen. She's there, and we'll get her then make them do what we want."

"She's not a dragon." Kirk told her that was all right too. She'd be easier to handle. "Yes, I can see that. We can knock her out better than a big man. You did say that they were big, right?"

"That's what Ross told me. And you said that Raymond had told you that they were as well. This might not be perfect, but once we get a dragon, jewels won't be far behind. We can work on getting the book and what it entails later. All right?" Mildred nodded. "Good. That's good. All right. We should go to bed now and rest up. We need to be on our toes when we speak to these people. I know that it's not going to be like anything else we've done to date."

"No, they'll be very suspicious of us. Not that I blame them, but after what Ross has done to them, this will be harder on us. Speaking of him, what should we do about him not helping?" Kirk told her that they'd deal with him before they saw the Mannings. "We can't have him telling on us. Yes, I like this plan. You're so good at this."

"I know."

As they readied for bed, he thought of the note again. Who would have taken something like that? And how did they get it all? It would have taken days to gather it all up, and that was if they could get a large truck down there. Which wasn't possible. He'd have to think on that tomorrow when he was rested. Whoever it was, he wasn't going to let them get away with this. It was their money.

131

~~~

"So, this plan that you have in place, you believe it will work?" Winnie told Hudson that it would work perfectly. "But you won't tell me what else is going on? You know something, and you feel that I'll be better off not knowing."

"Yes. I mean, I could be wrong." Hudson said he doubted that. "Okay, then I hope I'm wrong."

"You could tell me. I could help you with it." She didn't want to talk about it, and when she turned her back to him to look out the window, he seemed to understand. "We're having dinner with my family tonight. It's Simon's birthday and a big deal for us. His first as part of our family."

"I asked him what he wanted for it, and he said that he had everything he needed. I told him that birthdays are for getting things that he didn't need, but wanted." Hudson told her that was the right thing to say. "Yes, but I didn't get an answer. So, I peeked. He really does have his heart set on the bike that Cooper and Carson are getting him."

"Lucas and I went shopping for him some clothing. I know it's a lame gift, but he seems to enjoy getting new clothing. I think it stems from his mom being so broke all the time. Anyway, I guess you and Carson got him something as well." Winnie told him. "That'll be great. Tickets to the amusement parks when they open would make me happy."

"I got us some as well. Everyone passes, including Foster. I think we should make a nice vacation of it a couple of times." He thought that would be wonderful too. "I don't know a lot about buying for a kid. Any age. The younger one, John, he's easy. He tells me daily what he wants for his birthday. However, it does change with the wind. I think he's adorable. Simon is so serious."

"He is." She knew that he was watching her. Hudson

wouldn't interfere with her thoughts, but he would worry. "I thought that the two of us could go into town tomorrow and see about those buildings. Lincoln has his work cut out for him on the market place, and I want to help him."

"I'd love that." She would too. And they were going to have the faeries that didn't have as much to do in the winter months run it for them. The greenhouse was going to help a great many people, she thought. "Did you know that Rose and some of her men were going to help with the building? She said that as far as greenhouses go, she doesn't have a lot of knowledge, but Cooper got her a few books she can go over. For a faerie, she's very smart. I mean, like scholar smart. Few faeries can read, much less be able to do the things that she can."

"When her and Cooper came together, she was failing at a great many things. He would read to her, teaching her the words so that she might read them herself. After a while she learned math and other subjects with him when he'd go to college. I think at one time, she was even going to classes that dealt with the human body and the mind." Winnie said she could see her doing that. "I think that's why she's so good with her men. She has the knowledge and the experience that lets her know just how to make them loyal. Not to mention, she's a genuinely nice person."

The view from the window was of the yard beyond them. It was a nice place; the pool took up a great deal of the sunny area, and she wondered how much they'd use it. She much preferred the lakes and oceans for her fun, but thought a pool, without fish or salt, would be nice. Winnie thought about the summer months just so her mind would leave the problem she had alone for a time.

"I've never gone camping. I know that I've slept out in

the woods, even in caves for a time to heal or whatever, but to pack up a camper and to go someplace hasn't ever been a thing I did. I suppose that I was just too busy, but that sounds like something I think I could enjoy." She turned to him and he smiled. "Have you gone?"

"No. Like you, I've slept outdoors, but never had a vacation where I would travel for fun. Rarely did we do anything when we were trying to be more human. Once, when we'd been blending in, we did go to a carnival. I have to tell you, it was the worse experience of my life." She asked him why. "They had all these animals caged up, and some of them were shifters. When the thing closed for the night, Lincoln and I stole into it and let the shifters go. I don't remember his name, but one man said that he'd rather stay where he was. He'd been caged for so long that he wasn't sure how to be human anymore."

"That's sad. And heartbreaking." He told her that two of the people worked for the family. "Finny. And, let me think.... I know, it's Roger, the man that does your books."

"Yes on Roger, but Finny, no." He laughed. "She has a very checkered background, from what I've heard, and I've not asked what it was about. Finny is...Let's just say that I'm slightly afraid of her."

"You should be. She's been around the block a few times where men are concerned. I'd leave her be when she's in a mood too." Hudson said he'd do that. "I'm going to confront the people soon, perhaps before the end of the week. I'd very much like for you to be with me. And Cooper. The rest can go as well, should they wish, but I need the two of you there."

"All right." When he didn't ask her why, she nodded and turned back to him. "Winnie, you know that I'd die for you, don't you?"

"Yes, and I for you, but we won't have to. This confrontation, it's just that for now. It'll get nasty later, but for now, it's just something I have to do." He nodded at her. "I'm sorry. But I'm having enough trouble dealing with this as it is. And we must protect Carson. As much as she'll let us."

"Of course. And all of us will be there. For however you need us." She knew that as well. "Oh, and the stuff we found, Cooper has put it with the things that we got from our family. He kept it separate…he has plans to use it for other dragons. There was a great deal of jewelry too, that we're going to see if we can find the owners to."

"They're all gone, generations of them are all gone." He didn't say anything and she looked at him. "That's the reason I need him with me. Cooper will have to pass judgment on them. No one else can, not for the crimes that they committed on the dragons."

"Do you know the dragons' names?" She nodded. "And are there a great many of them? The reason I ask is because according the law, they'll need to have them read to them before punishment is set."

"I'll give them to him." Hudson stood up and took her into his arms. "You have to go. I know you do, but please be careful. All right?"

"I will, and you as well. When I get back, we'll go to Cooper's home and have a lovely dinner with cake and gifts, and not think about what else is going on." She told him she'd love that. "Good. I'll be back in a few hours. You don't work too hard."

She would, and she was sure that he knew it. When he left her, she sat back at her computer and stared at the names there. So many dragons had given their lives for this, and she wasn't sure what would be done for them. Cooper would

135

know, she hoped, but it was still heartbreaking to her that so many had given their lives in pursuit of the very ones that were going to kill them.

When Carson showed up an hour later, Winnie printed the list and gave it to her. She stared at it for so long that Winnie was ready to take it back. But when she looked at her, tears in her eyes, Winnie told her she was sorry.

"Not as sorry as these two are going to be. I'm going with you too. I know that you said it was optional, but I'm so going to be there when these names are read off. And the fact that they wanted the book too, something that does not belong to them, is the cause of so many of these names being on this list." Winnie told her that greed played a part in it as well. "It's always like that, isn't it? Greed and one-upmanship. I hate humans."

Winnie laughed and pointed out that she was one up until recently. "Not to mention, you've been around them most of your life."

"Yes, but I never realized this trait that they have. Anyway, I thought we'd go into town together, and then pick up Simon's cake. I know this great place we can have lunch, if you want to." She told her she'd love that. "Good. And I want to see the new buildings too. I heard they're coming along nicely."

They left twenty minutes later, riding to town in Carson's new car. She needed to get one for herself, she thought, just so she didn't have to be carted around all the time. Mentioning it to Carson, they added the car dealership to their list of things to do today. It was nice having a friend, Winnie thought.

Chapter 10

No doubt about it, Lincoln was in over his head. As his friend told him everything that he'd done to make his market work, he told him at least double that in problems that he'd encountered. Rubbing his forehead again, he looked up when Mick laughed at him.

"You'll be fine. Do you know how I know that? Because you have the funds already to make the smaller problems go away, and the big ones aren't that bad once the little ones are taken care of. They sort of equal things out." He asked him why he thought that. "Well, I didn't think I was going to make it either. The little things I was talking about seemed to pile up on each other until I thought I'd drown in them. Had I the funds, which I didn't have back then, I would have fixed them and they wouldn't have grown. You're doing this the right way. You, my friend, will be just fine."

"I have no idea why, but I believe you on this. I'm no less overwhelmed by it all, but I'm beginning to see where I can do this." He wanted it to work too, for the simple reason he hated to fail at anything. "I've got the building being brought up to code and having the water lines brought in, as well as heat. It was wired for gas lines a long time ago, so I'm going to use those when I can."

Mick pointed out how far he'd gone from an idea to making it work. "Even in the few days I've been here, I've seen real progress, and the townspeople think it's great too. Most of them have gardens around here, and would love the opportunity to sell their produce. I heard one group of ladies saying that they were going to grow different things than each other so they'd not be in competition." He told him he'd heard that as well. "And vendors will be coming out of the woodwork too. Just be careful not to let in too many of one thing."

"Yes, I read that somewhere too." He walked through the building again, marveling, as Mick had done, at the progress. "We're going to have room for twelve full time vendors in the middle at first. Then more if it works out. I'm having the building completed, but just the middle and outside areas will be used in the coming months. I didn't want to take on too much at once."

They had a butcher coming in that did his own beef and pork. A fishmonger that had direct contact with a fresh fish supplier. His brother had a fishery in New Jersey, and he was bringing some things to his brother for a while...just until they established if it was going to work out. Also, there were restaurants. Not as many as he had requests for, but enough to start the ball running.

"You have a good variety of shops, too. Sandwiches and subs will be a good place to have a quick lunch for the businesses. An ice cream shop for the kids, and I have to tell you, I'm looking forward to the spice shop you're having put in. That alone will bring in the business." He told him that Finny, his brother's cook, had come up with that idea. "Regardless, it's a good thing. Ours does a hell of a business."

There were other things going on too, things that Mick wouldn't understand nor have any idea of. Like there would be specialty shops for some of the paranormals around. Herbs for medical purposes. There was going to be a clinic at one end of the place that would have a class on what to do if someone's mate was human and they had to care for them. Things that he'd not thought of, but Foster had.

"They don't want their other halves to be hurt, but they might not have any idea how to care for them. Like medicines for a sore throat. Then there are labor pains. Heard tell of one man who nearly lost his missus because he didn't understand that she'd not heal quick enough after having his cub." Lincoln had asked him if that was common, to know those things. "Not on some of them older ones just finding their mates. You take you and your family, for instance. You expect me to take on some of the newfangled things around, on account'a I've seen them. I don't have nary a clue how to use them, I just look."

Lincoln had laughed for nearly twenty minutes about the television problem Xavier had had when Foster had turned it on and didn't know how to turn it off. When he'd gotten home that night, the sound was so loud that his ears hurt. Apparently, the elderly man had just kept pushing buttons until he'd been so frustrated that he'd gone outside until he'd returned.

Dinner was at the town's only restaurant. The proprietor had come to Lincoln a few days after it was announced what he was doing and asked to speak to him. He had an idea to put his salads, which people loved, in the place and sell them for lunch specials. Wallabies wasn't open for lunch except on

Thursdays, and he thought it would be a nice change for his employees and the people around town. Lincoln told him that he'd not see a problem with that.

After Mick returned to his hotel, Lincoln looked at the houses that were on his list to check out. There were four of them, all of them close to his family, but just far enough away that he could be alone when he wanted. Which was a great deal lately. As he and the realtor looked at the second house, he thought of how much he was working on making himself a recluse. Not really, but he was finding more and more excuses to not be with his brothers. It wasn't them, it was him.

Two days ago, he'd been invited to go to Xavier's home for dinner. The elderly man, Foster, had made chili, which the weather was perfect for. He told his brother that he had a million things that he needed to get finished for the visit from Mick, when all he'd really done was sit on the deck. Then yesterday morning he'd been invited to have dinner with Lucas, and then see a movie. He'd made up excuses then as well.

"Mr. Manning, there is a great deal of property with this house. More than any other in the area." He asked him how much there was. "Fifteen hundred acres. There are farmers who rented it out from the previous owners, but they know that the land is up for sale and are aware that new owners might not be all right with the arrangements. Also, years ago, it was my understanding that there were neighborhood plots on the land."

"You mean rentals?" He nodded. "That sounds like something that I might need. Where are they?"

They were far from the actual house, but close enough to the road that people could get to them without bothering him. But they were in poor shape. He would bet that it had been several years since anyone had planted anything in them, they were so overgrown. There were even a couple of pumpkins that had been left behind that were a pretty good size when the frost had hit them.

The third house had nothing that he liked. The owners had liked modernized things, a great deal apparently. Glass mirrors covered every wall space, as well as gold and brass doorknobs and cabinet pulls. Not to mention, nothing was natural. Not the flooring, which was kind of plastic, and there were heavy drapes on all the windows, which had at some point been painted black for some reason. They moved on to the fourth house.

"This house needs some work. A bit of updating, as well as a new furnace. The owners are no longer around. I believe that their children are trying to sell the place for a bigger profit than I think it's worth." Lincoln said that he'd been around when the house was up for sale a few years ago. "Yes, and sadly, it's not going to sell for the current price. The only good thing about it is that its fifty acres butt up against the land at the second house. I was thinking that whoever bought that house would purchase this one just for the acreage."

Lincoln laughed. "You old devil you. You knew that when we went there, didn't you?" Peter said that he had, but wanted to sell him on this house as well. "Why? I mean, what is it about this house that you want me to have it?"

"Not the house. Not really. It's too nice to tear down, yet the foundation is good enough that if someone did put the money into it, it would be a gem. A rental, I guess. If you were to purchase the other house with the land, you'd need someone to oversee it. This place has its own entrance, as well as it would be close enough to your land that whoever you hired to keep an eye on the place could easily go back and forth." Lincoln asked about the price. "You let me handle that. I can get it for a lot better price if they don't know the buyer. They'll hold out if they think they can get a dime more out of you."

"The owners…where are Mr. and Mrs. Jamerson now?" He said that the missus had passed away, but the mister had been put into a cheap nursing home. "If they won't play ball, tell them that I'll take over the care of Mr. Jamerson as part of the house. I liked the couple."

"Everyone did. But when the children found out about the housing boom around here a few years ago, they put them in that place so they could have control over the house and income. I don't think they realized they'd not be getting their parents' checks too to care for the upkeep on the house. It's a shame really, how some humans treat their elderly." He couldn't have agreed more. And knew that he'd care for their father anyway. "How about the house? You buying? I can make an offer today, and more than likely hear back by tonight. It's been on the market a long time as well."

"Yes, on both. And as you already knew, I'll buy the bigger house even without this one." He looked at the house again and spoke without looking at his agent. "The other farmers, are they up to date? I mean, there haven't been any issues with them, have there?"

"None. One of them grows corn, the other, he grows straw and hay. They help one another when the crops are due in. And I believe they hire some of the local high school kids to help every year. It helps pay for sports camps, as well as the band camp for a lot of kids." Lincoln said they could stay, but he had the option of taking the land back when he needed it with a year's notice. "Perfect. And I'll not tell them either who the new owner is. That way it'll be quiet for a while."

Lincoln drove over to his new home. He was going to finance it, to help the town. He wasn't sure how that worked, but Peter had said that it stimulated the economy with the bank having the interest funding. He didn't care so long as he wouldn't be bothered with making a monthly payment. Lincoln was going to have it set up so that the money simply came out of his account each month.

The house was in great shape. He loved the view from the back deck; it was nicer than the one at the apartment he was living in now. It was also without neighbors. Lincoln didn't have a pool, but if he decided that he needed one, he had plenty of money to put one in.

There was the matter of the barn that was attached to the land. It was in poor shape. The roof, which had long ago pulled free in a storm, was slate planks, and nearly all of them were busted in some way. There had been leaks too, damaging some of the wood in the walls, as well as the large ladder that led to the upper floors. Straw or hay had been left to rot, and the smell was strong when he first opened the doors. Walking around, he was amazed at the number of equipment pieces and hand tools that had been left behind. He'd have to ask Peter about it when the house was his.

By the time he was back to his apartment, he'd heard from Peter. The children of Mr. Jamerson had countered on the offer. He almost told them to go to hell, but Peter pointed out that if he didn't care for the funeral arrangements for the old man, he'd be put in a pauper's corner lot.

"It's not the taking care of him that bothers me, it's the fact that they're willing to write him off already. The man is their father...don't they care?" Peter said they more than likely didn't care at all. "Tell them I'll do this, but I want it all in writing. I don't want them coming back on me and saying

I fucked them over."

"You'll have it. Also, about the house and its contents. I made sure that the land and house are as is for both places. That way if you find something later, say a treasure chest full of money, it's yours as well. I did the same thing for your brother, Cooper when he bought his house." Lincoln asked him if he meant the treasure that was supposed to be there. "Yes. I know that people have been searching for it for years, but one might not know just where to look. Who knows?"

"Yes, who knows?"

So tomorrow, he was going to the bank to sign off on the paperwork, then he was going to move in. He didn't have much, certainly not enough to fill the place up, but he was excited to start this new venture.

He was going to ask Cooper if he could go through the warehouse for some of their things. Furniture that they'd bought and had put into storage. They threw away very little, then or now. Things, he knew, had a way of coming back into style, and for his money, Lincoln enjoyed the old hand-hewn things that his family had used a long time ago. He also wanted to ask him about the great desk that had been his when he'd been living in Europe a few decades ago.

Packing up his things, he was glad that he'd not made much of an effort to get things for the apartment. He had lived there for a number of years, but he rarely did much more than sleep there. As he was putting things into his truck, Lincoln felt excited for the first time in a long while. He hoped that he felt this way when he started putting furniture in the place.

~~~

Winnie watched them as they made their way to the local restaurant. They weren't being very quiet about how they were looking for a dragon. Nor that it was their dying wish to see one. So far, they'd been told to fuck off and that they were nuts. The restaurant had been warned, too, that they were broke.

"They have no funds to come here? I don't understand." She told the owner that they were going to try to play on their sympathy. Sort of try and con him out of a nice dinner for two. "Well, that won't work. Not even for an aperitif. I didn't just fall from the potato wagon."

"It's turnip." He said that he'd fall from where he wanted, and she laughed with him. "Just be careful. The male likes to hurt people. And the female will...she's very violent as well, but in a less physical way, and more mental. She could very well rape your mind hard enough to kill you."

He promised that he'd be careful. Sipping her tea, she wasn't surprised when Cooper sat beside her. Tonight was the big night for them all. Winnie ignored him as best she could.

"I have it all set up for you." Winnie thanked him. "And to let you know, the entire bunch of us are going to be there. I'm to understand that you've asked Hudson and Xavier to wait and be dragons when you need them. Is this necessary?"

"Yes, it is." She'd already talked to Hudson too. He knew everything. "The names, you have those as well? The Board is all right with you passing judgment on them?"

"I didn't even have to convince them of it. When I said that I had a list of the dead, they asked me if I'd take this one for them." She figured they'd not want to be in on this. "I did make sure that they put that in writing. Just as you said for me to do."

"They've been known to change their tune when someone comes back on them. It's happened to me a couple of times, and I've learned to cover my ass." He thanked her this time.

"Cooper, when this shit goes down tonight, I need you to stay focused on what they're going to do. It won't be nice or pretty when this comes down to it."

"You've talked to Hudson." She nodded as she took another sip of her tea. It was a wonderful thing, to sit in the cold with a thermos full of a hot beverage. She'd been doing it for the last few days. "He's upset for you. Not at you, but for you. Do you want to tell me what's going on?"

"I can't. I don't.... Please don't ask me this. It's been hard enough trying to get this all in a nice neat row." Winnie sat her thermos down and looked at him. "When I'm on a job, I don't just take things at face value. I dig and dig until I have all the information that is out there, then go over that several hundred times. Then when it's time for me to kill or to capture, it is without a doubt to me or anyone that I'm doing the right job. If I kill, it's because there isn't any way for them not to be guilty of whatever crime it is."

"It's why you didn't go after Ross. Nor Ford when he was alive. You knew there was more to it than those two men." Winnie told him she'd been right, too. "How long have they been at this? Killing dragons and paying men to come after us? I'm assuming that they're the first of the slayers, correct?"

"They are the reason that you've been hunted so much. Not to say there aren't more of them out there, but they are neither funded as well nor as well informed. For the most part, what is left are a few men and women who don't actually believe there are dragons, but don't want to take the chance that they'll miss out on capturing one of them. Understand?" He said that he did. "These people have been funding groups for a while. And when things start to die down, the sightings of them, they come up with a plausible story to generate interest again. Also, when they find a dragon and they have killed a few of them, they use their bodies to fund other interests that they have. Like murder for hire."

"Winnie, these people, you know them, don't you?" She looked away and nodded. "And you told Carson that they were after her. You know more than you've told us, don't you?"

"They killed your mother." Cooper didn't say anything and she looked at him. "I didn't know it when I began this chase. You should add her name to the list as well. I didn't before this because I didn't want you to…You might have done something that would have made it difficult for this to be justified. And we both know that it has to be right and legal, even though what they did wasn't."

"I think I might have figured that out. And like you, afraid to say anything. Does Hudson know?" She told him Hudson knew it all. "Thank you. And I would wish that you'd not tell the others, not until this is done. Okay?"

"Yes, and if you wish it, I can tell them." Cooper said he'd do it; it was his duty to his mom. "All right then. I'll meet you at the home of Ross later. He's not expecting any of us, but by the time you show up, he'll know why I'm there."

"Does he know what you are?" Winnie grinned. "I see. That must have made his bladder weaken. And his part in this, who gets the pleasure of giving him his punishment? I'm assuming that it's not you."

"No. Hudson has asked and he will do it. It's according to the laws too, where he'll end up. If he lives that long. He's sort of on the edge of life now."

Cooper stood up and put out his hand to her. "Thank you for everything. Loving my brother and keeping us safe. But mostly for being a friend. At first I didn't think we were going to make it, but I'm glad to see that you've had a change of heart."

"No, I still don't like you. But you have grown on me. A little anyway." When he left her there, laughing as he moved on, Winnie smiled. Things were going to get bad soon, and she couldn't wait for it to be done.

After the couple was run out of the restaurant, she followed them to the hotel they were staying at. She'd made arrangements with the owner there to wait before kicking them to the curb. Cooper had backed her up too, telling them that he'd pay for their stay, but not to let them know. Nor were they to charge anything to the rooms from now on. That had been easy, the manager said; they hadn't given him a credit card to pay for things like that.

Winnie ended up at Ross's house about an hour later, and found him just where he'd been for the last several days...in his office with the blinds closed. His clothing was dirty and he needed a bath. But it didn't matter to her what he looked like, so long as he played his part well. Winnie was sure he was going to do what she needed flawlessly. When confronted with a larger enemy, people with the kind of magic he had reacted the same way...begging for their life and making promises they had no intentions of keeping. Just what she needed him to do.

When Winnie sat down across from him, he stared at her for several seconds before he turned away. She wasn't bothered by his lack of manners; he hadn't had any for a long time anyway. Leaning back in the chair, she asked him if he was ready to face his crimes.

"Crimes? I don't know what you're talking about. How did you get in here?" She entered his mind and let him know she had the power to go wherever she wanted. "Ah, so you've finally come around, have you? What are you thinking that

I've done now? Nothing. You've known all my crimes for the last several days. And I've not done a thing since."

"No, you've not. But you will. You're about to have company." He just sat there. "Mildred and Kirk are coming. They've been trying to reach you for several days now."

"I've been busy. And why are they coming here? I've given them notice that I cannot get what they want. To see a dragon. That's all they wanted. You take them to see one. I'm to understand that you know a few." She told him he did as well. "Yes, fat lot of good it's done me."

"You mean the book." He glared at her. "As I told you before, we have it now. We got it from a man who's been dead longer than you have been alive. Well, you'll die soon, but he's been given a new life."

"Good for him. And you tell those people that I don't want them coming here. In fact, I don't even want you here." She just laughed. "I'm serious. I think you've caused me enough trouble. I had it all set up to get the book and one of the dragons to open it for me. Then you had to come along and fuck that all up for me. Do you have any idea what that sort of magic would have done for me?"

"Yes, it would have killed you and all of mankind. And every other living creature that is on this planet. It was never meant to be used for anything but to keep us safe. Opening that book up would have been the death of us all." He snorted at her. "You don't believe me?"

"Oh, I think you think you're telling me the truth. But I know for a fact that it was to hold all the riches in the world. All the magic that one person could handle. And I was going to be that person. Until you stuck your nose into it." The doorbell sounded and she smiled at him. "Why don't you just go away? And take them with you?"

149

"No, this ends tonight. So be a good boy, Ross the Black, and go greet your guests. I will be right behind you." She stood up and he did as well. This wasn't going to be any easier on her than it would him, but she had an advantage over him. Winnie knew what sort of couple was coming into this house; he had no idea.

Cooper was coming out of the dining room as she and Ross came from the office. The rest of the Mannings were seated in the living room, waiting. Foster was keeping an eye on the boys, still at home so that they'd not see what was going to happen here. While she knew it was going to be bad, she wasn't sure just how bad it was going to be. She supposed it would be up to Cooper. He was, for the most part, in charge.

Just as soon as Ross opened the door, she saw them standing there. They were younger looking than she remembered, but she knew that was mostly to do with the magic that they'd taken from the dragons they'd killed. Kirk was fussing about not being served any dinner, and Mildred was upset about the ride over here. Neither of them noticed her.

Cooper told them his name and what his title was, and both of them backed away. Winnie's magic made the door disappear; there would be no one leaving until she was ready. Then they saw her.

"Hello, Father, Mother. It's so unpleasant to see you again. I had hoped I was wrong and that you were both indeed dead. But it looks like I cannot be that lucky." Her father looked at her mother, then back at her. "You are in deep shit trouble here. And it is my pleasure to tell you that you're going to be punished to the highest extent of the laws."

Chapter 11

Hudson knew that these people were her parents, Winnie had told him that they were. He had a hard time making that work in his head. Mostly it was the way they acted, but he could see how she looked like her mother a little, and Winnie had her father's hair color. At least what he'd seen of it before Winnie stripped them of their glamour. He was glad for the last-minute change in plan so that he could be here when Winnie dealt with them. He was going to be her rock when she was finished.

He looked around the room, at his brothers and the rest of his family, and knew their shock too. It was as if they'd been waiting for something bad to be revealed, but not like this. Even Cooper, who had hounded him so much that he wanted to tell him, he looked like someone had hit him in the back of the head with a pole. A big one at that.

"Wendall, I don't think this is the least bit funny. What are you doing here, anyway? I thought we told you that you were no longer welcome in our life." She said that she'd not been in their life, but they had hers. Her mother huffed as she continued. "No, I don't think so. We would have noticed you being around. You are such a stickler for rules. You would have pointed out to us what we were doing wrong and made us pay a fine. How do you even know these people? They're not your usual kind of friends. Actually, you don't have any, do you?"

Her father looked at Hudson, then at the rest of them when her mother stopped talking. "What are you doing here? There some sort of meeting going on? We can come back at another time if this isn't a good time." Kirk pulled his wife along to the doorway had once been. "We've had some business with Ross here, but I can see that he's busy. We'll just come back tomorrow."

"You'll stay right where you are." Winnie looked at Hudson and he could feel her pain. "This is Kirk and Mildred. They have no last name...at least they don't have a legal last name. They are responsible for a great many deaths. The names of their victims will be read now. Cooper?"

His brother stood up and started with the first name. Not only were the names in alphabetical order, but they also had the dates of their death and what was done to them. Hudson had seen the list first hand, and knew that there were over two hundred names on the list. And the things that had been done to his fellow dragons had been depraved.

Hudson reached out to Winnie, asking her if she was all right. *I think so. I've just been so afraid of this for days now.* He knew the reason she'd been afraid, and no matter how many times he'd told her his family wouldn't reject her over her parents, she still suffered. *I told Cooper about your mom. He's not going to read her name here. He's going to tell them after this is done.*

Good, I think that is best. He looked at the couple who were complaining about being here. They were good at blaming others for what they had done. *When do I take care of Ross who looks pretty beaten about now?*

He's going to be a problem. I can't take his magic from him. He's not on my list, and he has a free pass should he ask for it. That's not to say that he's not guilty of things, but he'll bring up that you have no permission from the Board to end his life. If so, he will only be sentenced to a human prison. And that won't hold him very long. He'll still have his magic because they won't know about it. He had his plans, which had been approved by Cooper, in place for the man. *I need for you to stick to the plan that we have in place. But you may have to act sooner rather than later. At some point, he's going to realize that this is less about him and more about my parents.*

When the list was read and Cooper had sat down, Kirk stood up. Hudson didn't have time to deal with him right now, so told him to sit down and shut up. When he didn't do it, Hudson snapped his fingers, and was surprised when not only did he sit, but his mouth was taped over as well. It was fun, for the moment anyway, to have enough magic to have someone do what you wanted them to do. He turned to Ross. He thought that Winnie was right. Time to take care of the bastard.

"You are guilty of treason against dragons. You have conspired against them with these people and many more. Raymond Ford is one person that we have evidence that you killed. You profited from the demise of several other of our kind, and you have taken money from them, which makes you a full partner in all that they are found guilty of." None of which would stick if the man argued that he'd not known.

When Ross stood up, Hudson was ready with his comeback when he dropped to his knees in front of him. The

153

sword appeared in his outstretched hands a few seconds later. He glanced at Winnie when she moved to stand behind Ross. It was more than they had hoped for, him bringing this up now.

"I wish for death, sudden and without pain." He didn't know what to do, so again, looked at Winnie. She motioned for him to take the sword from Ross, which he did. "I have no desire to spend the rest of my days in the prison of the Dragon Board. I want you to end my life where I stand, without any hesitation."

"He cannot do this without the Board's approval, and you know it." Ross smiled at Hudson, then looked at Winnie. The look he gave her said that he'd known, but was surprised that she did. When she continued, Hudson held the sword in his hands. "However, you'll be happy to know that he has it. Asking for it was my idea."

He would die in the way he had asked. The sword that he'd handed over to her mate would be used for the killing blow, but Ross hadn't counted on them having any idea about the rule or for them to have asked for permission. He was so fucked. As he looked afraid then, her thoughts were confirmed. He had counted on them not being able to follow through on it.

"What? No. He can't know that." Winnie asked him why not. "I don't know. I just...I've changed my mind. I want to go to prison. You will have to let me go to prison now. I've asked."

"Too late." Hudson wasn't sure that he could swing the sword, but the look on Ross's face told him that if he didn't do it now, they'd all be dead. He had his magic and thusly could harm them all. Bringing the sword around, he felt it hit the man's throat, and when it came full circle he wasn't sure that he'd even touched him. Then the blood began to spill from the cut he'd made. His head slipped from his neck, eyes still wide open, on his face a look of shock. Hudson didn't feel bad for what he'd had to do. The man had done terrible things, and would have done far worse. As his body fell to join his head, Hudson felt the infusion of power, like a warm blanket. Ross's magic, good and bad, had come to him and Winnie.

Turning, with the bloodied sword on his shoulder, he looked at Kirk and Mildred. The looks they wore were priceless. Both fear and awe were written there, and he didn't care for it. Handing the sword to Winnie, he wiped his hand on the towel she gave him. Ross's body disappeared when Rose and her horde of men came into the room. Hudson sat down.

It hadn't been that hard, not physically, to take the other man's life, but it had hurt him in his heart. Again, not for the man, but for what he'd had to do to take care that no one else was hurt by his magic or evil ways.

Mildred and Kirk were led to the yard. The room wasn't going to be big enough for their punishment. Holding onto Winnie as Cooper and Carson stood in front of the couple, he could feel her strength and knew she was holding on as hard as she could.

"You are found guilty of breaking all the by-laws of our kind." His brothers, Xavier and Lucas, landed in the yard, their dragons in their battlement armor. Cooper continued as they circled the two killers. "As king of the dragons, I hereby sentence you to death by fire. You will be burned by the same flame that you worked so hard to extinguish."

"Wait, wait. We have a right to ask questions and defend ourselves, correct?" Hudson had been told they'd do this, and that they'd try and blame this all on their daughter. When

Kirk spoke, he stood up, but was ordered to get back to his knees. "I'm an old man. Can I not be dignified in this?"

"You mean like you did Libby? The dragon that you had chained in the mountain for her tears? Or perhaps like Jacob, the dragon that gave you his cave when you were without shelter or food." Kirk said that it had been Wendall's fault that they'd had to do this. "I'm sure you have your reasons for blaming her. Please, enlighten us."

Her father looked confused. It wasn't that he didn't understand what Cooper had said to him, but that he had agreed so readily, he'd bet. Few could realize when Cooper was being sarcastic.

"Well, she left us all alone to fend for ourselves. How were we to know that she was going to be making all this money and not share it? And her power. Not once did she ever come back and let us have a bit of it." He glared at his daughter. "You were a selfish person, Wendall, and I do hope that you will be a nicer person and tell these people what sort of family you left behind in misery."

"Misery? Okay, your misery was that you had a daughter like me." He said that was true, very true. "You beat me daily before I was able to fend for myself. And when I offered you money, you said to me that it wasn't nearly enough but you'd take it. And that I had to give you more each time I got paid."

"There was only one of you, Wendall, and two of us. How were we to eat and have a nice home on such little money?" Cooper asked Kirk if he had a job. "Well, of course I didn't. Why should I have worked when she had a job? You're not paying attention here. She left us when she was just a kid to go off and be something important to the Dragon Board. My wife and I didn't have any kind of special powers, at least back then. All we had we had to steal for ourselves. Is that any way to treat a man who helped in bringing you into the world, I ask you?"

"What kind of things did you do to help out with raising her?" Kirk asked him what he meant. "Just that. Other than being the sperm donor to her being created, what else did you do to keep her safe and out of harm's way? Did you make sure that she was fed every day? That she had warm clothing and boots in the winter months?"

"Where are you getting this kind of questioning? This has nothing to do with how she is at fault here. If you need answers for something, ask her about the magic that she has. Why didn't she share that with us?" Kirk looked at Wendall again. "You're not making this easy on yourself."

"You mean I'm not making it easy on you?" He said that there was that as well. "I have no intentions of making anything easy for you. You were warned, three times, that you cannot kill dragons. You cannot take what doesn't belong to you. And I know for a fact that you were visited, several times, by the Board to tell you that you were breaking the very laws that I was paid to enforce."

"You make it sound as if we treated you badly." She said that they had. "Come now, Wendall, you surely have forgotten all that. It was a great many years ago. And if I had to do it over, I might have been a good deal nicer to you. I mean, you can't hold what happened a long time ago against us, can you? Just help your parents out here."

"How?" He said he wasn't sure, but he thought that she could stand up for them. "No, I'm not standing up for you because I don't believe in anything you've done. To do so would make me as guilty as you are. Perhaps more so, since I protected the dragons."

"There you go. I knew you'd get around to it being your

fault." Mildred looked at Cooper with a smile as she continued placing her blame. "You heard her. It was all her fault. Had she done her job, even a little, then we wouldn't have been able to kill the dragons at all. This is all in her lap. She just said so."

Cooper looked at her then back at her parents. Hudson wasn't sure what was going through his head at the moment, but he knew that it wasn't going to bode well for the couple. They had broken so many laws that he was surprised that no one had called them out before this. But he supposed going after the king while Winnie was around could be the reason.

~~~

Cooper knew what he wanted to do; kill them both and be done with it. But the Board not only wanted them to admit to killing the dragons, but their part in what Winnie had become for them. Their neglect was what had made her work so hard at finding a way to feed and clothe herself. He looked at Rose when she landed on his shoulder.

"They have done a great many things to warrant this, my lord. Too many for them to think about being set free." He said that they fully expected that. "They do, but I have a favor to ask. It is for the Lady Winnie. She is heartbroken over this, and that you must be the one that punishes them. My men, they wish to serve her in this. For all that she has done to keep the dragons safe for us."

"They are to die by fire." She said that she could make sure that they did. "How would you do that? You will be harmed yourself."

"Nay, we will only make them suffer in ways that you cannot, my lord." He looked at Winnie and saw that she was indeed hurting. "Take her aside, and while you have her back to us, we'll take care that they no longer pose a threat to our kind or anyone. It is the least that we can do for her. Then your brothers, they'll make sure that the spot that they die on will be cleansed for whomever lives here."

"I should like to take her aside, as you said, but go tell her what you wish to do. I won't make her suffer more by learning later what was done to them." She nodded and he moved to where she stood with Hudson. "Winnie, Rose and her men wish to end this for us. For what they've done to them."

He wasn't sure she was going to speak. There were no tears in her eyes, but there was pain. Also, he could see how hard it was for her to stand there, waiting for whatever he deemed appropriate for her parents. When she put out her hand, Rose went to her and sat down.

"I know what they did to their mother, the queen. I wasn't there, but I know it. The story is as old as the rocks and trees here." Winnie told her that she was sorry for that. "There is no reason for you to be sorry, my lady. You were not there when this came about. You were not the Dragon Protector at that time."

"They need to be ended." Rose nodded. "I don't want to make Cooper do it. I feel I should be the one that swings the blade or whatever their punishment is. They're my parents."

"Nay, my lady, they are only the ones that birthed you for us. They did nothing that would make them be a parent to anyone, especially someone as good and kind as you are." Rose smiled at Cooper, then looked back at Winnie. "I was there when Saber was hunted, and saved by you."

"He was hurt badly. I couldn't do anything to save him." Rose said that she knew that, and Cooper tried to remember who that was. Saber was a name he'd heard before, but he couldn't place when. "His family, they are well?"

Cooper remembered then. Saber had been the watcher to the castle of dragons. It wasn't a building, but a cemetery for dragons. And it mattered little to the keeper if there was only a scale or a whole of a dragon, he cared for them as if they were his children. Cleaning the faerie rings when they needed it, replacing stones, if needed, with his own money and time. Saber had been killed one night while on duty, and his death had never been solved. He didn't remember reading his name on the list either.

"They are very well, thanks to you. The children of Saber have taken over his duties, and the mother is living well too. She has a lovely home again, thanks to you, as well as enough food and other items just as you promised her." Winnie looked up at Hudson, who kissed her gently on the face. Rose turned to him. "She saved the boys, his sons who were with him that night. They were digging a grave for your mother at the time. She saved them with nothing more than a stick and a flame."

"You were so young." Winnie told Cooper that she was six at the time. "Yet you were able to keep someone from killing them. We owe you so much."

Winnie looked at Rose, then at him. "If you would step down, my lord, I think that Rose is right. Her way of dealing with them is much better on all of us, but I have a favor to ask of you both. There will be no mention of them again. As far as anyone is concerned, they were just a couple that had done wrong and paid the price. I wish nothing to do with them."

"I can do that." Rose stood up, her wings fluttering behind her. "When they are taken care of, we'll rid the earth of even their scent."

Winnie turned and started walking away. Cooper watched her. He respected her decision as well as he might have his own. He knew this had to be hard on her; killing one's parents could never be easy, no matter what they'd done to you. But in this, he thought that she was only thinking of him, and saving him from having to do the deed. He looked at Rose.

"Make them suffer." She smiled at him. "Then you are to kill them however you wish. And remember this…they killed my mother. I want them to suffer badly."

"Yes, my lord. And before we do, I would suggest to you that you tell your brothers. Now, while they can be here and know that the ones responsible for her death, and that of your father too, are taken from the world." He agreed and went with her to stand with them.

He didn't have to say anything. They somehow knew. And when Lincoln asked if they had permission to take care of this for Winnie, he told them what she had said, giving Rose the honor of killing them.

"But I wish to mark them with my dragon." Cooper started to tell him he could when the others chimed in that they wanted to as well. This was something that he thought they needed, and he did as well. As soon as he nodded, the six of them, as their dragons, burned the two in front of them.

There was no need for words. They knew their crimes, what they had done, and now they were set to die. Cooper blew his first breath over them, burning their skin to just the blistering point. Their screams were loud, their begging louder. He didn't care. And when the others had done the same, they walked away with lighter hearts. This was what they all had needed.

An hour later he was in his office. He'd long since given up on trying to get some work done, and had only been staring at the walls since his computer had gone black. When Simon entered the room, he was glad for the distraction of his thoughts.

"I have a question." Cooper nodded but waited. The boy was a thinker, unlike his brother. John would talk your arm off and say hardly anything you could remember later. "I know that when we first came here, I told you that I'd never call you Dad, nor would I call Carson Mom. We had one and she died."

"I remember. And if you're asking me if I'm upset with you about that, I'm not. I never have been." Simon nodded but didn't speak. "You having any trouble at school?"

"No. I'm on the honor roll. I was always so far behind before...Well, we didn't have a lot of money, and Mom was really ill. We did the best we could." Cooper said that he thought they'd done much better than that. "I want you to adopt me, both of us do. And we want to call you Dad and Mom. Well, you Dad, and her Mom. I'm mucking this all up. Can I start over?"

Cooper nodded. Speaking, which he was sure he should be saying something, seemed to be locked away from him. As Simon repeated pretty much everything he'd just said, Cooper tried to think.

"Are you mad?" Cooper asked him why he thought that. "I don't know. You have this scrunched up look on your face. Like you're holding onto your temper."

"No...I'm overwhelmed, actually. And proud." Simon asked him of what. "You. Your brother. The fact that you came in my office and didn't have any trouble talking to me. Lots of things. Like I said, I'm overwhelmed. But I have to ask you a few things first. You can call me Dad anytime you wish. I'd love that. As for adopting you, are you having any trouble at school?"

He knew that they were. Not from the students—they were well liked—but from the teachers. Just a few of them, but it was enough. They weren't too keen on teaching the children of a wealthy man. They thought that they should be with their own kind.

"You know that we are." He nodded. "I'm here because of that, but not how you think. You didn't step in and take over. You didn't order anyone to treat us the same. And Carson...Well, you know how she'd be if she'd go there. But you didn't. The two of you let us come to you. And John and I think that was the best thing you could have done for us."

"You have no idea how hard it's been on Carson, or myself, not to barge in there and make them be nice to you. But as you pointed out, it would have done no one any good, especially the two of you." Simon told him there were times when he wanted them to. "But you do know that we would have had you asked."

"Yes, we know that. John and I talked it over, and we think that we'd also like to take you up on the idea of the private school. I know a couple of the pack, and they're doing better than our classmates are doing. And they're being prepped for college, I'm not." Cooper asked him what he wanted to be. "I'm not sure yet. I'd love to be a doctor, but I don't know if I could handle the pressure. Or an attorney. No less pressure, but I could help in ways that I might not be able to as a doctor."

"True. And you do know that when you're old enough to make decisions on your own, you will inherit your mother's estate. It wasn't much, but it's for you and John. Also, you'll be an immortal, same as us." Simon said he knew that as well. "That means that you could be both, if you wished. Or anything you want, for that matter."

"Yes, we know that as well. Not that we are in need of anything, but we have it." Cooper said nothing. He wasn't sure if Simon thought he was giving them too much or something, but he continued. "I want to be a Manning. I know that I'll never be a dragon, though I wish that were available, but I want…we both want to be Simon and John Manning. A strong, proud name."

"I can't speak for Carson—although on this, I think she'd agree with me—but we'd be honored to be your parents and for you to carry on our family name." Simon nodded, then stood and sat again. "When do you want this to start? I'm guessing that it's not as easy as it sounds."

"You'd be surprised." John came in carrying a file. He dropped several papers on his way in, and had to backtrack twice to retrieve them. He put the messy file on Cooper's desk and stood back. His grin was as infectious as his smile was. "This is the stuff you need. I think you might have to put it back in order, but we got all the paperwork you needed to adopt us. I filled out John's part for him, and mine is done as well. And we made an appointment with your attorney to get it down. The sooner the better, we were thinking."

"You're very sure about this?" Both of them said a loud yes. "All right. But you have to ask Carson. She'll need to be made aware of this too."

"We already did. She told us we'd have to talk to you. And so you know, she's all right with it too. Dad." It took him by surprise, the feeling he got from being called Dad for the first time. He looked at John when he came around his desk toward him.

"You can be my dad too, right?" Cooper said that he would. "Good. Simon and me, we started calling your brothers Uncle too, and Mr. Foster, he's our grandda. He's going to take us camping in the yard this summer, did you know that?"

"I did."

He was still sitting there, looking over the paperwork,

when Carson joined him. "We're going to be parents."

She stopped walking and stared at him. When she came the rest of the way into his office, he asked her if she was all right with it.

"Yes, but I thought that you'd been told about the other baby." He asked her what baby, not really paying that much attention to her, when a question came up on the paperwork he didn't understand. "What does it mean when it says we'll need to have our home inspected and people coming by."

"I'm not sure, Dad." He looked at her. She had said that oddly, and then smiled at him. "We're going to have a baby. You and I made one. We don't have to adopt it."

"Seriously?" She nodded. "I...A baby? We're going to have a real baby? I mean, I know that it'll be real, but we're really going to have a baby?"

"Yes. And yes, it will be a real one." She laughed at him as he picked her up and swung her around the room. "Oh Cooper, I love you so very much."

"And I love you, my darling dearest wife. So much that I ache with not being able to tell you in words how much." She kissed him and Cooper held her. "A baby. That will certainly stir up the pot."

Chapter 12

Winnie moved along the cave carefully. She knew that the dragon had come in here, but there had been one twist after the other and she wasn't sure where he'd gone after that. There were droplets of blood, but they were dried up and Winnie was sure that the dust that was everywhere was hiding the freshness of it.

Just as she was ready to give up and start at the mouth of it again, she heard the keening sound. The dragon had been hurt. He wasn't a large one, not nearly as big as the Mannings. But she'd been sent to help him. Just as she'd found him outside of here, three shots rang out and he took off for the skies. How badly hurt she didn't know, but she had been searching for him for the last two hours.

He was deep in the cave when she finally came upon him. As she moved closer, telling him her name and showing him her sigil, Winnie watched for others. They'd been known to be a pack like creature, so she wasn't sure if there were others around or not. The scent of his blood filled her nostrils, and that was all she could smell.

"I'm the protector of dragons, Wendall. Wendall Manning now." He lifted his head, and she could see the blood at his throat. "I can help you, should you allow it. I've the means to make you well again."

He roared at her, his spittle spraying all over her armor. It didn't make her upset; Winnie knew that pain could make a person, even a dragon, lash out when they had help. As she drew her sword, she moved it slowly toward the chain that had been around his hind leg. Someone had held him captive.

"I'm going to remove this. Just push your leg to me and I'll free you." He hesitated for a moment, then moved his leg toward her. "Good. Just don't move, I don't want to hurt you more."

Her blade sliced through the thick iron and he laid his head down. When he suddenly rose it again, she put her sword out and stepped in front of him. She didn't know what was there, but it had alerted him enough that he roared again.

"Who's there?" No one spoke, but she could hear them talking. Not really talking, but complaining. As the voice got closer to them, the dragon laid back down. Whoever it was, he wasn't afraid of them. As soon as the female, a child really, came into view, they stared at each other for a second or two before the child launched herself at the dragon.

"Are you hurt badly? I saw you go down and I came as fast as I could. Daddy doesn't know where I am, and I don't think I want to go back again." She fussed at the dragon, completely ignoring Winnie. "You need to care for yourself better. How are you going to be my prince if you're hurt?"

"Excuse me." The child looked up at her and smiled. She told Winnie that she was his friend. "I saw that. My name is Winnie. I've freed him from the chains. Do you know who did this?"

"My daddy. He said that he was going to make us rich, but I don't want him hurt." Winnie looked at the wound that was on the child, and knew a kind of rage that she'd not felt in a long time. "He doesn't like me either, but he tolerates me."

She said that in three long drawn out syllables, as if she'd heard it a great many times. Winnie was able to heal the dragon, but not the child. She was human, and in order to help her, she'd have to give her a part of herself. Without permission from Cooper, she couldn't do that.

Winnie reached out and told him what she had. *Is her name Matilda Craig?* She asked the little girl and she said that was her. *She's been reported murdered by her father. Supposedly killed by a dragon by the name of Waco. No one believes him, I guess. He's been talking about having a dragon at his beck and call for years now.*

From the looks of the wounds on Waco, I'd say that's about right. But the little girl is very much alive, and fussing at the dragon that I'm assuming is Waco. There is something else you probably already know. Her father had the dragon chained up, and told the little girl that he was going to make them rich. I don't think he's spent a penny on the kid. She's in need of some boots, as well as a coat. The one she has on now looks like it might have been her father's, it's so large on her. Winnie asked him what she should do with the child.

She'll have to go to the police department, then after that, I have no idea. She's not anyone that we can pull under our wing, not without causing an uproar.

I'd like to cause an uproar up his ass. Cooper laughed. *I'll take her back, but the dragon will be upset. I think they're protecting each other. He's pretty gentle with her.*

The noises from the entrance of the cave had her standing guard again. Winnie told Cooper what was going on, and he told her to be careful. Pulling darkness around the dragon and child, she told her to be quiet. The dragon nodded as if he understood what she needed.

When the man came around the opening of the room they were in, she knew that he was the kid's father, as well as the captor of the dragon. And he was pissed off. Winnie was glad that she'd hidden the child.

"Where the fuck is she?" Winnie said nothing, as the man couldn't see her either. Not until she was ready. "Matilda? Where the fuck are you, kid? Your mom and I are looking for you."

She could smell them both, the woman and the man. He'd beaten her recently too; the fresh blood made her want to kill the man, making him suffer in ways that she'd not thought she had in her. As he moved around the cave, and around them, the woman sat down on one of the stones. It was then that she noticed that she was large with child. The man made his way to her and the woman covered her head.

"Don't touch her." Winnie moved out of the shadows of her own making as the man drew back to slug the woman. "You try and hurt her and it will be over before you touch her. Back away from her."

"Where the hell did you come from?" Ignoring him for the moment, she asked the woman if she wanted help. "She don't want anything from you. Get away from my wife before I have you arrested for murdering her."

"Murdering her. She's sitting right here." He pulled out a gun and pointed it at the woman's head. "Do you really think I'm going to just stand here and let you murder this woman? You're fucking nuts if you do."

"You're going to get your skinny ass out of here and leave me to my business. I got a kid missing, presumed dead, and I won't hesitate to make her momma dead too." Winnie glanced at the dragon, who was slowly making his way to the woman. Winnie decided that he'd have a better chance of saving himself and the child than she would at the moment, and asked him to hide the child. "Did you hear me? I said to get out of here, and I won't hunt you down and kill you myself."

"You should know right now that I'm not alone." Winnie said it loud enough for the dragon to hear her. "My mate is here. He's a Manning."

The dragon stopped moving and looked at her. Then he did the most incredible thing…he wrapped his body around the child and moved deeper into the cave. That was a good idea, she supposed, but she did worry for the two of them now. When she heard Hudson, she told him that there was a gun and the man laughed.

"You must think I'm stupid, don't you?" She said she was pretty sure he was. "I don't think you have anyone with you. And especially not some mate. You're going to do just what I said and I won't hurt you too much. But I'm going to kill her; she's breeding me another girl, and I just won't have it. You fucking bitch, you're not going to mess up my plans."

Hudson came into the cave just as the man was pressing his gun to the woman's head, like he was trying to make her into some sort of bizarre art project by making it a part of her. Winnie didn't move, but she did keep eye contact with her. The next few seconds were going to be frightening, and she didn't want the woman to freak out.

"You don't want to hurt her. She's your wife." The man laughed and said that she was trash. "Not your wife? Then that makes things easier for her, don't you think? I mean, if you're dead, there isn't anything like messy paperwork to fill out."

"You think you're going to kill me? You?" He laughed again. "I'm not afraid of anyone. I've got the power of the dragon behind me."

"Well, you're right about part of that." He smiled and asked her what part. "You do have a dragon behind you."

The gun went off just as Hudson blew his flames at the man. He'd not kill him, or she didn't think he would, but he would make his life painful for a long time. Winnie reached for the woman just as she screamed. She'd taken a bullet to her belly.

"She'll be fine." She hoped so anyway. Winnie looked at her mate just as he changed to his other self. "Hudson, take her to the clinic, and now. I can deal with the aftermath here. She needs help."

When they were gone, Winnie called for Waco and the child. The dragon shielded the little girl from her burned father as he too left the cave to go to the clinic. Winnie sat down and regarded the piece of shit in front of her. He was unconscious and he'd live, but he was in deep trouble with a great many people.

After a time he woke. His screams echoed in the cave, so she cut him off. Not killed him, but the longer that she'd sat there, the more that she wanted to. And not make anything easy on him. As he regarded her, she told him what his choices were.

"You can go before the Dragon Board…that's your first choice. The second one is you go before the police. And before you think about spouting off that a dragon burned you or that I was here, no one will believe you." He asked her why not. "They think you're nuts. As crazy as a loon. I don't know if you're aware of this or not, but no one saw the dragon when you brought him to your home. Waco is much smarter than you are, and didn't let anyone see him."

"You lie." She just stared at him. "I'm going to sue you. You'll regret ever coming near me. When I'm done with you, you'll wish you were as dead as my wife and kid are right now."

"About that, I'm immortal. And you didn't kill your wife or child. They're both safe." He called her a liar again. "You really need to come up with a better insult. I'm not a liar, and you are in trouble here. Which is it you want to take on?"

"The Dragon Board has no say in what I can and can't do to my family. And that dragon? You said nobody could see it, so they got no say over me either." Winnie stood up and raised her sword. "What the fuck are you gonna do now? Cut me? You already burned me up, so there ain't nothing you can do to me now."

"Want to bet?"

The Board arrived with little fanfare and looked at the man. She told them what he'd done, including what he'd done to his wife and children. "He has made no wish to be tried by either the law of his kind or you."

If the Board members had names, she never knew what they were. Mostly they were just called that, the Board. She waited for them to answer her as she looked around the cave. It was large, even for the age of the mountain.

She'd been in caves, in and out of them her entire career as a protector, but there was something about this one that sort of made her feel at home. Like she'd been here a million times before when she knew that she hadn't. When this was done, she was going to explore things. There was something here that she needed to find.

"We shall allow you to take him to the police of his kind.

And you will have no more trouble with him either." She asked if she could know what they'd done. "He will tell them everything, including the dragon burning him, and they'll think him unstable. Nor will he be allowed to lie to them. The children and the mother, they are well?"

"As far as I can tell. The child, Matilda, she took care of Waco, even at the risk of getting harmed by her father." The man in black, always the speaker, told her that she would be rewarded. "Thank you. I'll see to them now."

Winnie made her way to the police station, the wounds on the man nearly healed, thanks to the Board. When she told them what had happened, that he'd tried to kill his wife and had injured her, he talked about how he'd do it again, killing her this time as well as the child. It was over for him even before it began. Winnie made her way to the clinic after he was arrested.

~~~

"You'll do it for me? You'll contact my sister?" Lucas said that he would and assured her that he'd make sure that she was able to get to her. The woman, Ginger Rice, had given birth to a six-pound little boy not an hour ago. He asked her about him. "I didn't want Walton to know it was a son. He would have done far worst to me than he ever did before. He threatened to chain me to the bed so that I couldn't abort it. Not that I ever would, but he scared me."

"He is going to have a little scar that he'll be able to tell his buddies about. But he's doing well. And your daughter, Matilda, is staying overnight too, just so the doctor can keep an eye on her. She is going to be just fine too."

Ginger closed her eyes as she held onto the little boy. He'd gotten nine stitches in his little bottom. Had he been head up, the doctor told him, he'd have taken it to the head rather than bottom. They were all lucky that Winnie had been there, or there was no telling what he'd have done to them.

Lucas slipped out of the room just as Lincoln was coming down the hall. "She your mate? I mean, I am ready for about anything at this point." Lucas said she wasn't his. "I'm going in now. If one of us is her mate, we can protect her better."

"The others have been in and out of there, with the same thoughts. She's not any of theirs either. So you testing the theory is good." Lucas followed his brother in, but waited by the door. He hoped that she was Lincoln's mate. He'd already fallen in love with the little girl, and holding the baby had given him all sorts of odd feelings. All of them good.

When Lincoln came out of the room without speaking to Ginger, he just shook his head. Oh well, Lucas thought, maybe she'd hang around for a while anyway. The two of them walked down the hall to the nurse's station and Lucas asked for a phone. He wanted a landline for this call, as Ginger said her sister wouldn't answer blocked calls.

"Hello, this is Lucas Manning. Is this Grace Rice?" She said that she was, what did he want? "Your sister asked me to call you. I'm at the hospital with your sister and her children."

"Are they all right? Did he hurt them again?" He said that he had and that they were all right now. "That bastard needs to be in prison, not out like he owns the fucking world. Tell her.... I can't make it there right now. I don't have the money."

"I can send a plane for you. Or ticket if you prefer. But our family jet would be faster and easier for you to get here." She didn't say anything, and he was worried that she was going to tell him that she'd wait. "Your sister really wants to see you, miss. She isn't going to pass or anything, but she needs to see you. And if it makes a difference, Walton Conrad is in jail for attempted murder of them both."

175

"He should be dead. And would be if I had any say in it. You really have a jet that you're going to send for me? Why would you do that?" Lucas told her that he was a nice guy and wanted to help a nice woman. "Yeah, well, if you're pulling a scam on me, I'm going to hurt you. I might not be all big and strong like you sound like you are, but I will hurt you. I'd like to talk to Ginger first."

"Of course." He gave her the number to her room. "She's resting right now, but I'd bet she'd love to hear from you."

After hanging up, Lucas laughed. She sounded so disbelieving of him that he had to laugh or be upset. Turning to Lincoln, he told him what she'd said and how he had to wait to send the plane.

"I'd send it anyway, just to have it there when she makes up her mind. Why are people so unbelieving of someone being nice to them?" Lucas said he wasn't sure, but thought it was the way of the world. "Yes, probably. I was wondering if you'd come over to my house for a little while. I have some projects going on that I need a second opinion on. And the garden areas for the high school kids."

Lincoln had bought himself a nice big house. It was bigger than he'd had in mind for his own, but it suited his older brother. And it had come with these plots, all marked out and ready for someone to use in the spring. But they'd been overgrown and the soil needed some work. He'd hired a bunch of the high school kids to help clear them off, and they'd mentioned that they'd like to use them for their end of year projects. Lincoln had agreed.

"They want to plant corn and such to see its effects on soil. Also, they have this idea to use their own compost, from the school's kitchen, to make the dirt stronger. After all the work they did on it, I just couldn't turn them down. And we ended up putting in a dozen more plots so that they could use them in the future."

"I like the idea. Are you going to be all right with a bunch of teenagers running around your land?" He told him that Simon was one of them. "Still. I know you like things calm and quiet. You might hate it after a while."

"Maybe, but I really did enjoy hanging out with them all the last few weeks. Spring is just around the corner, and they've already gotten me looking at seed catalogs and buying hoes. I also put in a water spigot for them. It wasn't that hard, and the well is fed from the mountain so the water is clean." Lucas asked him if he'd heard about what Winnie had found in the cave. "Yes. She and I are going there today to have a better look. She thinks that there might be more things in the cave other than the two cars that she found. She said the cave is speaking to her."

"Hudson is going too, I guess. I was asked, but I have things I have to get finished. Will you let me know what she finds out?" He said that he would. "I'm going to do as you suggested and send the plane on out there. It's not that far, a couple of hours by jet, but that's quicker than driving, I guess."

Lucas made his way to his own home. He had a lot to do today…he'd not been kidding his brother. He was in charge of making sure that their money was in good places to make more, and that contracts, whatever they might need read over, were okay. He had been an attorney at one point in his life, but he'd given it up some time ago. Lucas thought he might go back and get a refresher on some of the newer things.

He was just sitting down to his desk when Alan told him that the hospital had called and they were transferring a call to him. He was worried that it was going to be about Ginger.

"It's Grace. I'm going to take you up on your deal to get me there. I'm going to stay at my sister's home, if it's available. Ginger said that she wasn't sure who it belonged to, nor if the payments were up to date." Lucas said he'd look into it for her before she arrived. "She told me about the dragons, and that you and your family are ones as well."

"Yes. My family are all dragons, with the exception of my sisters-in-law. Does that bother you?" She asked him why it would matter to her. "I'm not sure, but you sounded sort of pissy about it."

"I'm pissy about everything. I'm not what most would call a people person. I don't care for them any more than they do me most of the time. It's Ginger that gets along with them." He laughed and she did as well. "I'll be there as soon as I can get going. I don't have a job that holds me down here, but I do have commitments. Did Ginger tell you about me?"

"No. She only said that she wanted me to contact you. Is there something I should know?" Ginger told him that there wasn't. "All right then. The jet will be there in as soon as an hour. I'll give you the information to contact the pilot. And there will be a car to pick you up. Just let him know."

"Thanks." Lucas said it was his pleasure. "You might not think so when I get there. I'm not going to change my ways just because I'm not at home. I wanted you to know that."

"I'd not have it any other way. And when you get here, I think you might be surprised to find out that we don't take shit from many people either." She laughed again and he leaned back in his chair. "Are you human?"

"Yes. Broke, poor, and trying to make a living plain human. I take it you're as rich as Midas and have all the shit in the world." He told her that he was comfortable. "Yes, I'm sure you are. Lying in your silken sheets, eating steaks every meal. I'm not complaining about how you're helping me out, but it would be nice to get a break once in a while. But enough about me and my woes. I'll be there soon."

He wasn't sure what he expected to find out about the woman, but he did a search on her name. Lucas was surprised to find out that she was a struggling painter, and that some of her work had been on display recently. Looking over her work, he decided that he wanted a couple of them and looked at her prices. No wonder she was struggling, he thought. She wasn't charging as much as he thought she could get off them.

In ten minutes he'd made two calls. One to buy the two that he wanted, and the second call to a friend of his, a shifter that dealt with artists of all media. Garrett Massey was an honest and good man. A tiger of the highest regard too.

"You dating this person and you want to get in good with her?" He told Garrett that women naturally loved him. "Yes, of course they do. While handsome men like me have to stand on the sidelines and wait for your discards. What does she even look like, this paragon of...? Holy shit, Lucas, she is good."

"I told you." He listened to his friend as he went through the pictures that had accompanied her showing. "I've purchased two of them. The one called Red Dawn in the Morning, as well as Midnight. And her prices are too low. If I like these as much as I think I will, then I'm going to purchase two more."

"Not until I'm finished with her. Christ, they're beautiful. And you say that she told you she was broke? I can see where her prices are well below what I'd want them to be, but this, she should have commissions for all sorts of work. I'm going to give her a call as soon as we get off here." He told him that she was on her way here. "You old devil you. What would you have done had I not taken her on?"

"Called someone else." Garrett told him he'd better not. "I'm not now, but it's not what you think. Her sister is here, and hurt. I've arranged for her to come and visit her sister and stay a few days. She said her work is portable. And after seeing this, I'm going to set her up here in town and see if I can persuade her to hang around a few more days."

"You do that, but I'll pick up the tab on this one. My God, man, she's going to be a millionaire." He was sure of that. "I'll be there tonight to see her. You can put me up, can't you?"

"No, I don't like you that much." They both laughed. "Yes, I can. You know that. And while you're here, I can show you a few projects I have going on with your money. I still can't believe you talked me into being your broker."

"I've never been more confident in anyone in my life. You have already made me money. I'll see you tonight, my friend."

Only time would tell if this pissed her off or made her happy. He had a feeling, either way, she was going to bust his chops. Smiling, he wondered if she was his mate. Lucas felt protective of her. As he made arrangements for the extra bedroom in his apartment to be cleaned out, he wondered what she'd think of his family. And realized he didn't think she'd mind at all. Grace would certainly fit in well enough with the women.

Chapter 13

The cave was deeper than she thought it would be. There were so many twists and turns in it that she was sure had they not marked the way they'd come, it would be forever before they'd be able to get out. She looked over at Hudson when he said her name.

"I feel it now." She said she did as well. He looked at his brother. "What do you feel? Anything yet?"

"Yes, I feel like you've scammed me into coming down here so that you could leave me for dead." He turned to the path in front of them and took two steps before stopping again. "Wait. I do feel it."

"What is it?" He said that he didn't know, but Lincoln looked into the path to the right and told her there was more light that way. "We could cover more ground if we split up, but I don't want to be stuck down here either."

They'd been at this for a couple of hours. They'd followed the light that seemed to be getting dimmer as they moved, but when she looked down the same path that Lincoln had, she could see that it was indeed brighter.

181

Hudson said it was his turn to lead and she let him. Lincoln was at her back. The two of them had been guarding her for the last twenty or so minutes. While she didn't need them to do that, Winnie was glad for the extra care they were giving her. Hudson came to yet another fork in the path and turned to the two of them.

"I think this isn't a fork off from the main, but a combination of the two of them. The light is just as bright in both of them. And it's stronger here, whatever it is." She agreed. "We'll go down the right, and come back here if it goes nowhere."

The caves were huge. Even the paths off from the main cavern had been large enough for their dragons, should they need to be one, to stand tall in. Winnie had brought flashlights with her, as well as several paint cans of spray paint to mark the paths that they took so as not to get lost. She was glad now that she'd also brought snacks and water. This was going to be a project.

So far they'd found two cars dating from the earlier century. And there had been a suitcase in one of them with names and pictures. She didn't want to think about why it would have been inside it, but because of the dampness of the place it was in, the car was rusty beyond anything she'd seen. The second car, much deeper in the caves, had held a body. Even she could tell that it had been a self-inflicted gunshot to his head. Most of it was gone, but the gun in his hand was still there.

They had also found some places where larger animals, a bear probably, as well as some large cats, had been staying and living for a while. Not for a long time now, but they had used it for their lair. When Hudson stopped walking, she bumped into him and started to tell him again to warn her when she looked where he was.

182

"Holy fuck." Yes, she thought, that about covered it. Lincoln moved ahead of her and stood next to Hudson. "This is beautiful. And well preserved. Look at the books over there."

Someone had made this their home. And she'd bet anything that whoever it was, they were still around. There wasn't a bit of dust on anything. The fire in the hearth, made entirely of stone, was smoking. Before either of them took a step into the home, because that was what it was, she stopped them. Pointing out what she'd seen, she waited for them to tell her she was wrong.

"Who is it, do you know?" She didn't, and told Hudson that as he whispered his question. "I'm guessing by the amount of magic we can all feel, that it's someone powerful. I can't get a reading on who it might be either...I mean, what sort of nonhuman they happen to be."

Winnie couldn't either, but started to back away when she saw the person she just knew had lived here as long as, if not longer than, she had been alive. She saw them as well, and motioned for them to come down to her level. Going down the stairs, she told the men to be ready and they said that they would.

The woman wasn't bent over with her age, her spine as stick sharp as her own. Her hair, as black as some of the areas in the cave, hung down below her feet and dragged over the floor. Her gown, dark too, was covered in the front with a white apron, as stark a difference as night and day. And she was very powerful, just as they had thought.

"Hello, Wendall. These must be the Manning dragons. My, how you have grown up." She didn't touch either of them, for which Winne was glad. "You don't remember me, do you? None of you? Well, I can't say that I blame you much.

183

It has been a very long time. I'm Satie. Your uncle and I, we were good friends back in the day. And I was the one that gave your father the mixture and spell to change you."

~~~

Cooper wasn't sure what to make of any of this. He had too much going on right now, and he was feeling slightly dazed by it all. His boys were doing fine. Carson was feeling pretty good, and he was out on a limb so far he was terrified of concentrating on any one thing for fear of it breaking under the weight and leaving him hanging.

"You all right?" He nodded, then shook his head. "Yeah, I was feeling that too. If you're worried about Winnie and the other two, I'm sure they're fine. I heard from Hudson a little while ago, and he told me that they'd found a house like place in the cave and they were talking to the person there. I guess she's some sort of witch."

"In the event you thought that might help, it didn't." Cooper looked at the stacks of files on his desk that needed his immediate attention. "I'm in over my head. And I get more and more over it every day. I can't seem to concentrate on things I need to do because I'd rather be with you guys. Not that I'm blaming any of you, because you tell me I need to work. But you guys are amazing, and I love spending time with you."

"I have told you to hire someone to help, but you have to be the big man on campus and do it all on your own. What's the big deal? Hire someone, train them to do what you want, and move on." He said it wasn't that easy. "Yes it is. I'll show you how easy. Ginger is going to help you. She and her baby and daughter are going to be staying here for a few days, and she feels like she needs to do something to repay us. And she needs a job."

Ginger came into the room and smiled at him. He liked this woman, and had fun with her little girl and holding the little boy. Waco was currently watching over the three of them because he said he owed them his life. Ginger sat down and told him her experience.

"Before Walton came into my life, I was a secretary for a doctor's office. I mostly did filing and input. I've also scheduled appointments, answered the phone, as well as done spreadsheets for him when he needed to upgrade his offices. The bank said that I did a fantastic job, and hired me on to help out with other businesses that needed a plan. I can and really want to do this for you. Carson said that you weren't keeping up." He glared at his wife, then smiled. It was the look she gave him that had him entertained. "I won't tell anyone what you are. I haven't told anyone about Waco."

"I know that. And I trust you not to." She nodded. "But this is very complicated. I have to go over the proposals for the new stores downtown. There is also the income sheets for all the rent that is due that has to be deposited as well as filed. Then I have...What are you doing?"

"One thing at a time. Give me the proposals and I'll fix them on a spreadsheet for you and bring that to you. While I'm doing that, you can check off the rent for the people, as well as tell me what account you want the money in. I can either do it online or, if you want, go to the bank. I have a car now."

"I told her that while she was working for you, she'd have transportation." Cooper nodded as Ginger gathered up the files she needed. Carson handed her a small scrap of paper before she left the room. "This is the passwords, as well as sign on to the computer. You have already gotten clearance from the bank to make deposits. Right now you can't take money out, but if this works out, we'll change that for you."

Ginger left the office and Carson took the chair she had been in. "You knew that she can be trusted?" Carson said that she'd had her checked out. "And what else can she do besides get me flush with all this?"

"She speaks three languages and can read them. That alone can help you with overseas projects. Also, and this one is going to really impress you, she's an accountant. Does taxes as well. She's a whiz with numbers." Cooper asked her why she'd done this. "Because you won't. And I'm lonely with you working in here all the time. What else can I do to help you?"

"I have so much going on at the moment. I should have had a meeting with the Board three days ago. Then there is the auction that is going to be held to raise money for the prom for the kids." She told him what Lincoln was doing with the gardens. "I heard. They want to know if it's all right if they put up a stand too, to sell off what they grow. I approved that right away."

"Good. Also, I went to the meeting at the library that you had set up. They called and I asked if I could do it for you. I think I'm going to take that over...for me, not you." He told her to have at it. "Anyway, they're going to have a booth at the fair this summer, to sell off some of the books that they have too many of. I think they're also looking for donations and food to go along with it. They need a new computer."

"How many did you buy for them?" He laughed when she turned red. "I'm glad that you're doing this. I hate going there. They have tea and cookies, and the cups are too small for my big hands, and I'm terrified of breaking one of the chairs."

"Well, I have it now." Cooper looked down at his list of things he had to do and marked off two of them. There were still a lot of them to go, but he was feeling less overwhelmed by them. "Okay, what else I've done. I've taken care of the gardens around the school. They are going to get fresh flowers, as well as some herbs. That was a request from the principal. Since it's all the same to me, I said okay and have set up the purchase of them, as well as the planting."

"The spreadsheet is finished." He was shocked by that and asked Ginger if he could see it. "A few of the bids were from the same company, so I put the lower number on here, but made a notation on the bottom of what the second amount was. And the names of the buildings are across the top of the sheet. Since I didn't know where they were, I left that blank so we could fill it in if you think you need it. I was able to put in the addresses on a few of them, so you'd know what I was talking about."

She took the rent checks and the book he recorded them in, and asked if she could computerize it. It was like having someone in his mind, getting it done just the way he wanted it. He was still sitting there, dumbfounded, when Carson snapped her fingers in front of his face.

"Are you all right?" He said that he was in shock. "Why? Because there is someone out there that can do your job faster than you?"

"Yes. She couldn't have been gone any more than twenty minutes, and I have it in my hand. Did you give them to her in advance?" Carson said that she'd not done that. "Carson, I've been putting this off for weeks, maybe months, and here it is all done and I'm getting our rent money put into the computer. Why didn't you do this before?"

"Because you kept telling me you had it. Besides, I have to make you suffer a little so that you appreciate everything else I do for you." He said that he did, very much so. "Now, what else? I don't want you to be stressed out anymore. The baby doesn't care for it."

"I'm sorry. Come here and let me tell her how sorry I am." She said it might be a boy. "I don't care so long as it's healthy and looks like you if it's a girl. A little boy might suffer if he was as beautiful as his momma."

He held her for as long as he could, telling her how much he loved her, but his business was getting done and he felt like he could work on it now. When she left him, Cooper got to work. For some reason it went better. Knowing that he had help certainly put everything into a different light for him.

By dinner time he'd narrowed down his list even more. Ginger had left him once to nurse her little boy, but he was getting so much more done he wasn't even afraid anymore. As soon as she returned, he gave her the permission she needed to take money out of the account to pay bills for him, and handed her the checkbook.

"There are several invoices that need to be paid, as well as donations that I make monthly. If you could please set something up so I can be reminded of those, I'd appreciate that too." She told him that she knew that the bank would automatically take the money out and pay whomever he needed them to. "Good, then set it up. I can't thank you enough for this. I don't know what I'd do without you right now."

"You might change your mind when my sister gets here. She's my twin, by the way. Gracie is sort of caustic when the mood suits her better than being nice." He asked her when she was getting there. "I thought yesterday, but she has something that she needs to finish. Something about a man wanting to see her work while she's here. Your brother, Lucas, he told her to take her time and load it all in the jet to bring. I don't know what's going on with that, do you?"

"No, but if Lucas is involved, she'll be fine." He asked her what Gracie did. "I'm assuming that she works from home?"

"A painter. That's what she calls herself, like she paints houses for a living. Not that it's not an honorable job, but she's more than that. She paints these amazing paintings, and they're really good. I hope that this person can see that when he talks to her." Cooper asked her if she knew the man's name. "Yes, it's Garrett Massey. Do you know him?"

"Yes, he's an art dealer and critic. If he's asking to see your sister's work, then she'll be a hit in no time. He owns and operates Massey's. Heard of it?" She said that she hadn't, but she didn't go out much or read many newspapers. "You should look him up. Perhaps talk your sister into letting him represent her if he wants. He's that good."

"You've not met Gracie yet, so I'll let you know, if she doesn't want to do something, there is no talking her into anything. She's very stubborn." Ginger smiled sadly, and he wanted to hold her, like he did her son. "She told me to come live with her and hide from Walton. Even before...Gracie told me that he was bad news, and that I'd be better off getting a restraining order on him. But he...Walton is stubborn too. And mean. He kidnapped me. For about a year now he's kept me in his house and I couldn't get away. I've never told anyone that before."

"I'm so sorry." She nodded and walked to the window of his office. There were spring flowers poking through the last-minute snow they'd gotten last night. "Do you want to talk about it?"

"Yes. I think I do." She didn't look at him as she continued. "Matilda isn't his. Walton hated her. But he used her to get me to do things that I wouldn't normally have done. He kept me chained up, you see. Her too. Just as he did that poor dragon. He did that to me for a year and a half. For eighteen months, I was never allowed to just move where I wanted. Do anything other than to cook and clean for him. And sleep with him. When he found out that I was having another girl, he got meaner, and would only allow me out of the house when he was with me. I guess so I'd not run. But he kept me in line by threatening my daughter. He'd actually hold a gun to her head until I complied with whatever he wanted. I think...I have no idea how she attached herself to that big dragon, but he protected her when he could. They had a bond that even beating her wouldn't break. And Walton did try everything. Then one day they were both gone. I was frantic with worry, but somehow knew that the dragon had her. That she was safe."

"How did he know to go to the cave, did he tell you?" She told him. "Tracker. I don't think I would have thought about that. It was on his shackle, you say? Well, Waco—that's his name—no longer has to worry about that, not while he's here. Walton was going to kill you both, did you know that?"

"Yes, he told me daily that he was sick of me, and Matilda. And when he put the gun to my head that day, all I could think about was her being safe. Then that woman, Winnie, came out of nowhere and saved us. You have no idea how much I owe her."

"Much like your sister, I don't think I'd tell Winnie that. She'd just say that she was doing her job or that he deserved it. She does protect the dragons, but I think she was happy she could help you both too." Ginger told him it was three. "That's right. I don't think I've gotten his name as yet. Have you decided?"

"Yes, she's going to hate it too. I've named him Wendall,

after her." They both laughed. It felt good to both of them, and Cooper could see that she was in a better mood too. "Anyway, I can do what you need. My children are well cared for. My sister will be here soon, and I'm free. Thank you all for that."

"It was our pleasure. And you can't imagine how happy I am that Carson brought you here today. I got more done in the few hours you were here than I have in a month. Thank you." She nodded. "We'll talk about pay and benefits tomorrow. I haven't any idea what the going rate is for someone of your caliber."

"Whatever you pay me is fine. And Carson said there was insurance as well as the car. That is going to be very handy." He said that it would include whatever she wanted. Then Rose came to him, sitting on his desk after he introduced them. "You're very pretty. I hope you don't mind me working for your dragon."

"Nay. I hope you do not mind, but I have sent some of my men to watch over your children. They are safe here, but I think they thought it a boon to be able to play with and watch over them. There are no babies here as yet." Rose eyed him, then looked at Ginger. "You will have one as well. I would like to find one that can go to your home. That way, you can have a little help, magically, when you leave here."

"Thank you. I would like to say that it's not necessary, but I think I'd enjoy that as well. Waco, he'll be safe here too, I'm told." Rose nodded. "Good. All right. I have more work to do, and then I'm going to play with my son and daughter. Thank you."

When she left, Rose turned to him. He could tell there was something bothering her, and he waited. She was not one to be rushed, and he wasn't worried that she'd not tell him the absolute truth either. When she was ready, he turned his

191

monitor off but not the computer, and watched her pace.

"The witch is one that I know." He asked her what witch, then remembered Carson telling him about the one in the cave. "Yes, her. She is very powerful, and trustworthy, but powerful. She...she is the one that created you. The magic that made you what you are, my lord."

Cooper wasn't sure what to say to that. He'd never thought of her much after he and his brothers had been in the human world for a while. He had wondered, he supposed, where she was or if she still lived. But to know that she'd not only been found, but she was fairly close to them as well....

"Has she been watching over us? I mean, does she want something from us?" Rose said that she doubted it, she had all she wanted or needed. "Then why now? I'm guessing that she's been just sort of waiting for one of us to find her?"

"I don't think so. She could have come to you whenever she wanted." He nodded, still reeling from the knowledge. "I knew that she was around, just not where, my lord. I would have told you so."

"I know that, Rose. But I can't help but think that she will want something of us. Some sort of, I don't know, payment." She said that his father had paid her and paid her well. "I'm worried. I have children to think of. My brothers too. And any mates that might be on their way here. Christ, I wonder if Ginger's sister is one of their mates."

"I don't know that either. I do know that she is coming soon." Cooper got up to pace now; he wasn't just worried, but afraid. "I've only told you in the event that you want to make her welcome. And you should. She has given you and your family a great deal. Yes, she was paid, but it cost her as well. I have heard that she had to rest for a great many decades because of the magic that she gave your father."

"I'll welcome her, but that doesn't mean I can't take precautions too." She said that she'd expect no less of him. "Have your army watching her, in shifts, so that she'll not know."

"She'll know." He figured that too, but he was still going to do it. "And I have taken the liberty of asking more wolves onto the lands. You should let the pack master know that she is about."

"I will. Anything else you can think of, just do it. I want us to be safe."

After Rose left him, he sat at the computer again. He wasn't behind as much as he had been, but there was a lot to do still. But his mind kept drifting.

He did wonder if he was going too far in getting ready for her. Not just in military mode, but also in making his home more welcoming to her. For all he knew she could have been watching over them the entire time they'd been here, plotting and planning their demise. Shaking his head, he tried to dispel the notion that she was only out to harm them, and tried to think of more positive things.

It was well after seven when he left his office to find Carson and his kids. Something more was needed to distract him, and he knew them to be the perfect foil to his terrible thoughts.

Before You Go...

HELP AN AUTHOR

write a review

THANK YOU!

Share your voice and help guide other readers to these wonderful books. Even if it's only a line or two your reviews help readers discover the author's books so they can continue creating stories that you'll love. Login to your favorite retailer and leave a review. Thank you.

AWARD WINNING, BESTSELLING AUTHOR

Kathi Barton, winner of the Pinnacle Book Achievement award as well as a best-selling author on Amazon and All Romance books, lives in Nashport, Ohio with her husband Paul. When not creating new worlds and romance, Kathi and her husband enjoy camping and going to auctions. She can also be seen at county fairs with her husband who is an artist and potter.

Her muse, a cross between Jimmy Stewart and Hugh Jackman, brings her stories to life for her readers in a way that has them coming back time and again for more. Her favorite genre is paranormal romance with a great deal of spice. You can visit Kathi online and drop her an email if you'd like. She loves hearing from her fans. aaronskiss@gmail.com.

Follow Kathi on her blog: http://kathisbartonauthor. blogspot.com/

www.ingramcontent.com/pod-product-compliance
Lightning Source LLC
Chambersburg PA
CBHW032135170626
46808CB00006B/2247